The Rebel Christian Publishing

Copyright © 2024 A. Bean

All rights reserved. No part of this publication may be reproduced, distributed, or transmitted in any form or by any means, including photocopying, recording, or other electronic or mechanical methods, without the prior written permission of the publisher, except in the case of brief quotations embodied in critical reviews and certain other noncommercial uses permitted by copyright law. For permission requests, write to the publisher, addressed "Attention: Permissions Coordinator," at the address below.

ISBN: 978-1-957290-54-6 (eBook)
Print: 978-1-957290-55-3

This is a work of fiction. Any references to historical events, real people, or real places are used fictitiously. Names, characters, and places are products of the author's imagination. Inclusion of or reference to any Christian elements or themes are used in a fictitious manner and are not meant to be perceived or interpreted as an act of disrespect against such a wonderful and beautiful belief system.

The Rebel Christian Publishing LLC
350 Northern Blvd STE 324 - 1390
Albany, NY 12204-1000

Visit us: http://www.therebelchristian.com/
Email us: rebel@therebelchristian.com

Contents

1	1
2	10
3	17
4	33
5	43
6	56
7	70
8	79
9	90
10	98
11	109
12	124
13	135
14	144
15	159
16	177
17	189
18	199
19	208
20	220
21	235
Epilogue	248
More books by A. Bean & TRC Publishing!	253
ACKNOWLEDGEMENTS	255
The Rebel Christian Publishing.	256

The Gap

A Christian Age Gap Romance

By A. Bean

A Rebel Christian Publishing Book

1

Constance

Long Time No See

I'm officially a divorcee.

It sucks. But mostly because I was forced into this divorce. I'm in emotional limbo right now. My husband of five years—we've known each other for eight years total—told me he was in love with someone else and no longer felt the spark between us. Don't ask if I tried to argue my part because I did.

I told him his reason for wanting a divorce was dumb, and I didn't take him seriously until I was served with papers at my job. My secretary burst through the door, making a scene about special papers from my husband. Of course, I was in the middle of a meeting with a six-million-dollar deal on the line. Thankfully, I still managed to sign it.

My business is a liaison company. Basically, we are the guys who finalize deals between two companies/parties. Let's say a grocery store wants to buy half the land from a farm owned by a frozen food business. The grocery store would then reach out to my corporation to ask me to settle a deal with the frozen food chain. If we do our job right, we can get the best price possible.

I'm pretty much a glorified lawyer with a high retainer fee, but that's what happens when you're good at making deals. Unfortunately, this talent is a double-edged sword in the office since this business was built by my husband and me together. Now it's the ultimate showdown. Everyone wants to know who the better deal maker was between the two of us.

My husband wanted out of the company and out of the marriage. I didn't want to do either since that would wreck the company's funds and my personal wallet. Fortunately, I sat on the paperwork for too long and made him antsy. I was served with a *second* set of divorce papers three months after I didn't sign the first set. This deal was more reasonable since he dropped all the way down to half his original asking price.

My husband's eagerness was enough to hurt my pride since I knew he was chasing another woman. I wanted to make him wait a little longer, but I was afraid I'd wake up one morning and all the company's funds would be destroyed because he took his money and ran.

So, I settled on a payout. Half upfront, the rest in increments for fifteen months.

I got to keep everything except his favorite Porsche. I didn't care. I'd been planning to sell everything anyway. I didn't want to keep anything we'd had together.

My whole life was being washed down the drain with the

single stroke of an ink pen. It wasn't fair. After all our time together. After every Sunday I spent thanking God in church, why did this happen? God hates divorce, so why didn't He block mine? I prayed hard, but my husband was more relentless than I was. My prayers weakened and I eventually stopped praying about it and gave up. I submitted to defeat, but it was easier to blame God than to admit to my own loss. I know it's wrong and I'm trying to get my head straight, my heart back right with Him, but I told you, I'm in emotional limbo.

Now I'm nine months into this divorce and I owe just six more payments to my ex-husband. As far as the great debate goes... Who was the better deal breaker?

It was a tie.

Neither one of us was better than the other at making deals. Though, if I'm honest, I didn't care about any of that. But I think I'm the worst deal maker. I was gambling with him. Taking his low-ball wager in the hopes that he'd get angry, come back to the house, and we'd make love and realize how stupid all of this was. But that's the kind of thing that happens in books and in movies, not in real life.

In reality, my ex-husband ignored me. He left one night in his Porsche, and I haven't seen him since. I called him to argue, but eventually he just hung up on me. I decided to give him space, and then I was served with papers.

I'm such an idiot...

The thought swelled in my head like a balloon as I pulled onto the valet parking ramp. Tonight, I'd be having dinner with a client who'd been handled by my husband. I still haven't found someone to replace him, so I've doubled up on work. It's exhausting, but at the very least, I'm making more money since there's one less person on the payroll, and he happened to be a large paycheck. I, of course, got a pay raise, setting me as the highest paid employee at the company. And the most important employee. Yay.

"Excuse me," I called out the window to the valet worker. He wasn't the usual worker at this restaurant. The usual guy never made me wait in the car. I'd pull up and get out, and he'd take care of everything else. But this guy—rather, this *kid*—decided to make me wait while he took care of other clients.

"Excuse me!" I called again.

He glanced over from the other car and held up a finger. I sighed and leaned back into my seat. It wasn't a huge deal since I didn't want to meet with this client anyway. I knew all he'd want to do is ask for juicy gossip about the divorce. But I didn't have any gossip since my ex stopped speaking to me completely.

With another sigh, I checked my watch and looked back up at the kid. He was opening the door for a tall man with brown skin, a bald head, and wearing a long coat. His coat looked familiar; white trimmed in gold fur that came to a peak right before touching the ground.

"Danny had one just like that," I said as I watched the man move around the car.

He opened the door and a woman stepped out. I gasped. *That* is *Danny*...

I moved before I knew it. Scraping for the car door handle, I shoved it open and tried to climb out the car when my seatbelt tightened, lurching me and the car forward. In a frustrated manner, I ripped my seatbelt off and tripped out of the car.

"Danny!" I screamed.

He and his date both stopped walking.

"Danny!" I shouted again.

I missed him… seeing him suddenly weakened me. I just wanted him to come back. Who cared about the money? Who cared about the stress this divorce put me through? I'd do it all again just to prove that I loved him.

Slowly, my ex-husband turned to face me. Big broad shoulders, lovely brown skin, thick muscles. He was strong, Danny was the strongest man I've ever known. He looked… amazing. He was standing there with a woman holding his arm the way I used to. Clinging to him with eyes filled with love— the same love that'd once filled my own.

They were looking at me now. The woman on his arm had everything I had. Cocoa skin, plump lips, and even the same kind of figure, except mine was homegrown. This woman was manufactured from head to toe. Plastic cheeks, plastic boobs, plastic hair—what did he want with this girl?

"Constance," his voice was low and humming as usual.

"Danny…" I smiled and stepped forward, but he held up a hand, stopping me in my tracks.

"Joseph didn't tell you? He's meeting me tonight; it was kind of last minute."

I blinked. It took me a moment to understand what he meant—that my client had cancelled his meeting with me in favor of meeting with my ex-husband.

Before any of this could sink in, Danny started talking again. "My fiancée and I are starting up a new company. Better and stronger than yours."

"What…?" The question was still on my lips when he turned with a shrug to usher his fiancée inside.

"Fiancée!?" I screamed behind him. "That hussy is nothing like me! You think you can leave me and take my business too?"

Daniel whirled around and thundered down the stairs back to where I stood beside my car. I could feel everyone's eyes on us, but I didn't care. I wanted my husband back; I'd take the momentary embarrassment for a lifetime with him.

"If you ever speak about Jada that way again, it'll be your worst day ever. I'll take everything from you and leave you like the garbage you are."

"How dare you?" I snarled as I leaned forward. I could smell his cologne. He was still wearing the one I bought him for his birthday. The memories of us together filled my mind, and I nearly broke right there in front of him. Shakily, I reached for the car door.

"You out here causing a scene, and for what?" Danny went on. "We're through, Constance. There's no getting back together." He adjusted his jacket and looked me over, his anger finally softening, if only for a moment. "You need to leave. There's no reason for you to ruin our night."

Something inside me **withered**.

"Your *night?*" I shouted. "You ruined my *life*! And for what? Daniel, I'm your *wife*! You can't do this to me."

"*Ex*-wife!" Jada hollered from the sidewalk.

"Jada!" Daniel turned and yelled at her, but I shoved past him.

"Who do you think you are? You think you're going to walk around here as the new Mrs. James?"

"Constance! Get back here!" Daniel reached for me, but I snatched my arm away as I raced over the sidewalk.

Jada hiked her dress up and stepped down to confront me, but the valet kid got between us, and pulled me back.

"I'm Mrs. James! I will *always* be Mrs. James!" I screamed hysterically.

"*Please!*" the kid called over my shouting as he pulled me along.

"Get her out of here! She lost her mind!" Daniel yelled as I was dragged back to my car.

"You can't do this to me! Daniel, please!"

The restaurant entrance began to blur as I was dragged back to my car, kicking, and screaming for Daniel to come back to me. He casually placed his large hand on the lower back of his new fiancée, and he walked her into the restaurant without looking back at me.

"Ma'am!" the valet kid shouted as he pulled me around the car.

Reality seemed to slap me back to my senses. I suddenly became hyper aware of myself, of the sweat dampening my brow, of my racing heart, of the people staring at me, and of the valet kid's grip on my arm.

"Get off me! Stop touching me!" I hissed as I ripped free from his grasp.

"Ok…" He held up his hands, as if approaching a wild animal. "I just need you to get in the car, ma'am."

"And go where?" I whined as I stood there.

The valet kid's eyes were wide, and his breathing was heavy from wrestling me down. "Look, lady, I don't know where you can go. But you got a nice car and I'm sure you got a nice house. So just go home."

"Hey!" a man honked his car horn. "Call security or something! But get this crazy woman out of here so the rest of us can eat!"

"Crazy," I muttered… then I snapped. "*Crazy?* I'll show you crazy!" I slammed my car door shut and moved around to the back.

"Ma'am!" the valet kid yelled miserably.

My fist pounded on the top of his car. I didn't care about the heat or the pain rushing through my hand. "You think *I'm* crazy!" I yelled.

"Get her out of here or I'm calling the police!" The man in the car cowered and motioned for the valet kid to do something.

Fearlessly, the kid grabbed me as he begged, "Please, ma'am!"

For some reason, his desperation sent me spiraling into madness. Yet another man had had enough of me. And this one was a complete stranger.

I sank into a screaming fit, knees wobbling, tears blurring my eyes. I was going crazy, losing my mind as I was shoved into the passenger seat of my car. The valet kid got into the driver seat and sped off as I wailed beside him.

2

Joaquín

Picking A Side

"Listen, lady," I said as we drove aimlessly through town, "I know you're really sad and stuff, but right now, this is cutting into my—"

"I never thought I'd see him again," she cut me off, which made me snap my vision toward her. She stared straight ahead, the city lights twinkling off her tears. I'd just gotten this gig through my dad's friend. The Palace was short staffed, so they were looking for help in every area, and I got the job. It pays really well just for valet, so I can't imagine what the pay would be like if I actually worked *inside* the restaurant. But this whole thing put my chances in jeopardy. I didn't know what to do.

"Why?" the crazy lady went on. "Why would he do this to me?"

"I don't think I'm qualified to answer that."

She sniffled, adjusting in her seat to blink out the window. I felt bad for her; truly, I did. But this new gig had been hard to come by and I couldn't afford to take any risks. We had strict rules about doing favors for patrons, but I didn't know what else to do. Security hadn't shown up yet and things would've gotten a whole lot worse if I hadn't stepped in.

I glanced at her as we slowed to a stop at a red light. She had on a white pants-suit with a lace corset beneath it. From the way she dressed, and that screaming match from earlier, I gathered she'd been making some kind of deal and needed the extra push, hence the open jacket and lace corset.

I've been working this job for five months and have picked up on a lot of things. We think rich people are so different from the rest of the world, but they're not. They have affairs, they have cheeky ways of making deals, they're honest and they're liars. The big difference is that this woman's corset was probably a thousand dollars minimum, whereas a regular woman's corset might cost fifty bucks.

I glanced at the woman again, stealing glimpses as the streets whipped by outside. Her rosy lips were pouted as she stared off in silence. The hum of the engine was the only noise in the car. She was hurting, obviously, and I had no idea how to help her. I sighed as I pulled off the road. Throwing the car in park, I turned to her, but she spoke before I could say anything.

"What are you doing?" Her voice was clipped, edging the line of anger.

"I don't know where to take you. I'm just trying to get you

home."

"Just hit the navigation, it's in there as the most recent destination."

I nodded and tapped the screen. A welcome screen came on before fading into the navigation system. "This first address looks like a business address," I said.

She rolled her eyes. "Then pick the next one."

"Listen, lady, I'm just trying to help—"

"You said that already," she loudly interrupted. When I blinked at her in confused anger, she crossed her arms and stared out the window. "I'm sorry, ok? I just..."

The car fell silent, and I watched her cover her face, shoulders shuddering as she began to cry all over again. I tapped the screen without saying anything else and pulled away from the curb. Judging from the navigation system, it would be a long drive in awkward silence, but I had plenty to think about, and so did she.

"Alright," I said as I pulled up to her house, well, her *mansion*. "Do you want me to park this somewhere?"

"No, I'll park it in my garage in the morning." She discreetly wiped her nose with the back of her hand and then gathered her things.

"Well, ma'am, I'll leave you to it." I opened the car door, but she called out to me.

"Hold on, how are you going to get back to work?"

I shrugged. "Do buses run out this far?"

"Yes, there's a stop a few blocks down but—"

"Perfect. I'll get over there then." I checked my watch and nodded. "I should make it back with an hour left on my shift."

"Absolutely not." The crazy lady waved a frustrated hand and got out the car. "I will not have someone's mom calling me in the morning because her son didn't make it home."

I couldn't help but snort. "Nah, I'll be fine. Thanks though."

"I can't let you just walk away." To my complete surprise, the woman walked around the car and placed the keys in my hand. "Take the car back."

"I can't do that." I shook my head, meaning every word. This sounded crazy, and plus… a kid like me with a car like this? I didn't stop myself from speaking my mind. "Everyone will think I stole your car."

She thought a moment. "Just park it somewhere else, then. I don't care."

As if car theft was just a minor inconvenience, she waved her manicured hand and started up the stone steps to her mansion. It was one long rectangle with windows lining the entire first floor. It had a very modern look; sleek and fancy like I'd expect from a woman driving a Rolls-Royce.

I waited by the car until she made it to the front door. She turned and gave me a wave before walking inside.

Now that I was alone, all I could do was groan and rub my neck. If I took her car, I could just return it in the morning. If I didn't take her car, I'd run the risk of missing the rest of my shift. It was an aching decision, but I knew it was better to take the car, even if it was just for the night.

I tossed the keys back and forth in my hands, weighing my options one last time. Again, I came to the same conclusion. So, with a frustrated grunt, I got into the car and locked my seatbelt in place.

Rolls-Royce, Bugatti, Mercedes, Pagani—name any kind of expensive car, German, Italian, American made, what have you, I've driven it and parked it over the last five months. Some say my job is a privilege, being around old money, young money, and expensive things, but it's just a job for me. My mama raised me to be impressed with miracles, not materials.

"God," I said aloud as I drove back to work, "I have no idea why I got caught up in this mess today. I hope this is all part of Your plan, because my boss is not going to be happy when I get back."

And he wasn't.

When I returned, I realized my coworker, Jimmy, had been trying to cover for me, but there was a car pileup because of the spat earlier, and we lost a lot of higher-end customers who didn't feel like waiting for valet. Reservations were cancelled after the fiasco, and my boss swore that woman, Constance Wells, ruined his guest's night and his reputation. She might've made a few guests angry, but I didn't think she ruined The Palace's entire reputation. That seemed a bit dramatic.

"And then you drove her home? You were on her side? What is wrong with you!?" Mr. Adams was yelling at me in the backroom after I told him my side of the story and explained why I drove up in a shiny Rolls-Royce—which I hadn't stolen. He asked me about that, in no kind or few words.

His big furry mustache wiggled as he lost his temper, but it gave me a little entertainment while I stood there getting chewed out.

"You had better thank God I know you're a good worker, and your dad and I were very close before your mother passed or you'd be out of a job, do you understand me?"

I nodded.

"I need an audible 'yes,' Joaquin."

"Yes, Mr. Adams."

"Good. Now you want to tell me why you drove that woman home?"

"Things were getting heated, security was slow, and if I hadn't done something, the mess would've prolonged. I was just trying to do the right thing."

"Next time, consult someone about the 'right thing' to do." Thick sausage fingers made air quotes. "Now it looks like The Palace took a side! It looks like we're in on their spat—do you know how bad that is?"

I did, but I shook my head because I knew he'd tell me anyway.

"What happens with our patrons is none of our business! We always remain neutral!"

I nodded, and his mustache wiggled as he glared at me.

"This could have cost us serious money!"

He was yelling now, but I kept a straight face, glancing off from his hot glare, looking at the pictures on the wall. My dad appeared in a few of them, posing beside women and men with drinks in their hands. I've never met the other folks in the photos.

My dad and I used to be pretty close, and he shared a lot with me about his past before my mother died almost three years ago. Now we don't speak much. I don't mind his new girlfriend, Shelley, mostly because she never tries to act like a mother to me, but sometimes I wonder if three years would be long enough to get over someone I loved. I try not to think about it, because what do I know about love? I've never fallen into it, so I've got no clue how easy it is to fall *out* of it or move on from it.

"Keem!" Mr. Adams grunted.

"Yes, sir!" I looked over from the pictures to find him sighing in disdain.

"You're not listening. Just go and take the day off tomorrow. I don't want to see you until your next weekend shift."

I blinked slowly. "Will I get paid for missing work tomorrow?"

He squinted. "Seriously?"

"I kind of need the—"

"You should've thought about that before you took off in a Rolls-Royce! You should be counting your blessings I didn't *cut* your pay! Now get out."

I nodded, defeated. "Thank you, Mr. Adams." Then I left as he waved me on to the door.

3

Constance

Two Strangers

I called off the rest of the week. I couldn't bear the embarrassment waiting at the office. Not only had Joseph stood me up, and I found out my ex-husband now had a fiancée, but that same ex-husband shifted gears to try to take my business from me.

It made sense; I just hadn't realized it. But maybe I was wrong. Maybe Daniel James wasn't trying to take my business. Maybe he really was a better deal maker than me.

"He tricked me, Keesha," I said as I paced the floor in nothing but a silk gown. "He tricked me into thinking I wore him out with taking so long with the paperwork."

"Yikes," Keesha said over the phone. "Girl, what are you going to do? Because, right now, that man is living much better than you. He's got a fiancée—first of all—and now he's taking your clients? How many do you think he has?"

"I don't know." I jammed my thumb between my teeth and began gnawing on the acrylic nail. "I thought he was just asking for half because he was tired of waiting. But he was asking for half because he didn't need any more than that! So, there's no telling how many more of our clients he's already taken or how much new business he's got going on right now."

"You know people always trusted him more than you."

"Keesha," I stopped pacing, "whose friend are you? Because I don't think you're mine right now."

"I'm just saying," she said dramatically. "Constance, all this time he's been the one making the bigger deals. You've made good ones too, but you know he was the big gun."

"And he's counting on that." I moved over to the window and stared out at the pool in my backyard. I forced myself not to remember the endless nights Danny and I spent relaxing out there. We'd spend the afternoon soaking until we were wrinkly, and then we'd sprawl out on matching towels and let the evening sun bathe us in its warmth.

"Since you know that," Keesha's voice alerted me back to reality, "what are you going to do? You've brought in some heavy hitters, and you can swing a good deal, but those guys at the bigger companies are going to be looking for Danny or someone with his rap sheet."

"But I've made big deals too." I shrugged, turning away from the pool. My bare feet slapped against the cool tiles as I crossed the foyer to the living room. "And I made a lot of them with better terms."

"Yes, but his clients received better pay. You know

companies don't care about the fine tuning. If you're going to save your business, you've gotta do something soon."

"I *know*," I cried as I flopped down onto the couch. "This is the worst day of my life."

"Yeah, usually the second day is the most embarrassing."

"Keesha!"

She burst into laughter, which made me chuckle for the first time today. Keesha had been my closest friend since high school. We went to college together and I ended up joining her church during my first semester. We even became roommates for a while until I married Danny. So, Keesha's been there for everything. For our first date, for our wedding, for our business, and our recent divorce. She's really the only family I have here in California.

"Kiki, what am I going to do?" I said quietly, almost as if the question had just hit me for the very first time. Like I'd just realized I was truly divorced and truly out of options except to move on.

Keesha sighed. "You're going to get up, get out of whatever nightgown you have on—"

"How'd you know I was wearing a nightgown?"

"It's the lavender one that's got a silk bodice and plunging lace neckline." Her voice was so flat, I couldn't even be shocked.

"I feel like you're spying on me."

"I'm not." She laughed. "You're just a typical twenty-seven-year-old divorcee."

"How do you know that?" Dragging myself to my feet, I

exhaled heavily.

"Because I know everything," Keesha said matter-of-factly. She went on to name all the weird things I did when I was upset, things only she would know with all her experience as my best friend, but I wasn't paying attention anymore.

Out of my living room window, I could see a powder blue Rolls Royce—*my* powder blue custom Rolls Royce—pulling around my fountain out front and parking at my front door.

"Keesha, I've gotta go," I said, interrupting her.

"What? Why?"

"I gave a car away last night but now it's back. So I've got to go figure this out."

"You gave a *car* away? Were you drunk or angry?"

"I don't drink, you know that," I said as I jogged to a bathroom on the first level and grabbed a guest robe.

"I don't know, girl. You've been crazy lately."

"Whatever, Keesha. I'll call you later."

I hung up the phone and stashed it in my pocket as I raced around the house back to the front door just as the doorbell rang.

I took a breath and pulled open the door.

"Hey." The guy standing on my front steps had dark shaggy curls. He was handsome, to say the least. Big and tall, broad shoulders with a striking physique—which he showed off in his sleeveless fitted shirt.

I must have been staring for too long; when my eyes snaked back up his frame, one of his dark brows was arched in a silent question.

"I'm sorry," I said, nervously pulling my robe closed. "Do I know you?"

"Uh, yeah." He licked his lips and glanced over at my car. "You let me borrow it last night." He pointed a thumb over his shoulder. "And I came to return it."

"I'm sorry? I don't remember letting you borrow my car."

"You good?" he asked, his light brown skin crinkling on his forehead. "Because you were really adamant last night about me getting home."

I backed up and looked him over once more. "No, I let a kid, the valet kid from The Palace, *he* took my car."

"That's me." He pressed his large hands into his tight chest. "I'm Joaquin Ramirez."

"No…" I shook my head. "I don't remember you. You're not him."

"Lady," he said, and his voice sounded the same as last night. If this was the same man, he looked different outside of his uniform. It was baggy on him, and he looked more like a kid last night than he did today. Today, he had cheekbones and dimples, a jaw line to kill for, and facial hair like a real man. A little on the chin, a thin stache, paired with big brown eyes; this kid was night and day, literally.

"Listen, I wasn't going to bring it up, but last night I had to wrestle you into your car because you and your ex-husband got into a fight over his fiancée named Jada. And then—"

"Alright!" I held up a hand. "I get it, you're him. You just look different."

He chuckled, and it was a scratchy throaty chuckle, like he

was slurping his laugh between his teeth. "I get that sometimes." He shrugged. "I think it's the light or something."

I raised a brow. "So you drive women home a lot, I take it?"

"Nah." He stepped back, a fluid motion with a wave of his hand and a smile on his face. "I just mean a few people who are regulars at The Palace have caught me on the morning shift and said I look different too. I think it's just the rush of the night or something."

"Right, but you look…" I paused just to look him over once more. He was an attractive kid, but he *was* a kid, and I was way too old to babysit. Besides, I had a business to save and an ex-husband to get over. I didn't have the time for someone else, or the room in my heart right now.

"I look like a kid. I know." He smiled. "But I'm going to be twenty-one this year."

"You're *twenty*? Goodness, you *are* a child."

He frowned. "How old are you?"

"You never ask a woman her age." I crossed my arms.

"You're just a girl," he sneered.

"I'm a *woman*," I corrected. "And I won't let you ruffle my feathers."

He laughed, head back and stepping backwards a few steps until he regained his footing. "Alright, Miss—"

"Constance Wells."

He nodded. "Ms. Wells, you are definitely a woman, and I'm sorry for ruffling your feathers."

It wasn't a sincere apology, but I couldn't care less. I just wanted him gone.

"Here," he offered me the keys, "I just came to return your car."

"I told you to keep it."

"I know, but I can't afford the insurance and all that. Besides, I'd rather you just give me some cash since I was suspended a full day of work because of you."

"What?" I snapped.

He stood there nodding and shaking the keys in his hand, not even looking at me. I didn't know if he was bothered by being suspended or not—he really didn't seem like it—but it was my fault regardless.

"Well, fine, I'll give you a day's wages."

"A day's wages after I was suspended? You can only get suspended, like, twice before you're *fired*."

"Ok, so?" I shrugged.

"So, I got a suspension because of *you*. You've gotta pay for that suspension."

"Are you seriously making me pay for your *suspension*?"

"Yeah," he said flatly.

I scoffed. "Incredible. I gave you a *car*. A very expensive car."

"But I returned it."

"And I'm paying for a full day, and you got to use my really nice car for an entire night."

"I went back to work and home. The stupid car caused me a mound of problems anyways. I live in a bad neighborhood." He slipped his hands back into his pockets. "I literally had to hide the car off somewhere and sneak out the house early to bring it back here. So you should really pay me for my troubles too."

I grunted loudly. "You're a terrible person, you know that?"

He smiled. "So, my day's wages, my suspension, and a little extra for my troubles."

"All of this for one car ride home?"

"I did a lot for you," he said dramatically, "I rescued you from a fight, drove you back home, got suspended for you, hid your car, brought it back while knowing I *need* a car, and I protected your reputation last night at The Palace and this morning when reporters bombarded me while I picked up my check." He crossed his arms, thick muscles flexed beneath his thin tee. "I think what I'm asking for is reasonable."

"You ... protected me?"

"Yeah." He jerked his head in a nonchalant nod, like this was no big deal. "Only because that Danny guy is a real jerk. I don't even know what happened, but I don't think either of you handled it right. Still ... it's not fair for you to get all the blame."

"Is that... what you told reporters?"

"More or less. Fair is fair, that's what my mama always taught me."

I chewed my lip as I glanced off. I thought he'd make fun of me just like everyone in the office will when I return. But this valet kid, who really doesn't owe me anything, stood up for me. During the divorce, everyone at my *own* company wanted Danny to win (except for Keesha and my secretary) even though they never said it. They didn't have to say it to my face. I heard all the rumors going around that Danny was so great, and that it was no surprise he wouldn't want me anymore since he was stronger on his own.

It was hard to hold my head up every day with all that drama screaming in my face, but I tried not to let the chatter bother me. However, standing here, looking at a kid who had more sense than my entire staff, made me want to break down and cry in relief.

"Can I offer you a drink?" I blurted without thinking, and then—so he wouldn't get the wrong idea about this *drink*—I quickly added, "Do you like iced tea?"

He looked surprised for a moment, and then he asked, "Why are you offering me tea and not money?"

I deflated. "I just ... I want to talk to you. But I'd prefer to do it inside."

He took a step back and looked at the entire house before his eyes landed on me. "Alright, but you better not be trying anything funny."

"No," I waved, "I just want to talk."

"Alright." He bopped his shoulders up and then down and casually followed me inside.

Taking him through the foyer, we traveled to the kitchen where he ogled all of my high-end appliances as he sat on a white highchair. The island had a pink and white marble countertop that matched the bright marbled floors. He was looking around as I grabbed a glass from the cabinet and poured him a cup of iced tea.

"Do you like it?" I asked.

"It's tight," he said with a nod.

"I designed the entire house myself." I passed him a glass and took a sip from my own glass.

"You don't have any workers? Like, someone to clean this whole place?"

"*Housekeeping*," I corrected—the word *workers* sounded so old fashioned, but he didn't even seem to notice my input. "I've got housekeeping," I repeated. "Usually, they're not here when I'm here. They come when I'm working, and are gone before I come home, so I don't really see them. They'd be here now, but I called off work and told them not to come in."

"Gotcha," he said as he took a sip of his tea. His eyes bucked and he stared at the glass, quickly swiping a tongue over his full lips. "It's good," he said, holding up the glass to closer inspect it.

"Homemade. Fresh lemons, handpicked tea leaves, and cane sugar make all the difference."

"Fresh ingredients." He took another sip and then hummed into his glass. "*Dang*, it must be nice to have that kind of food and drink every day."

I shrugged. "You get used to it, honestly."

"Really?"

I nodded.

"So, what did you want to talk about?"

I set my glass down and stretched my hands across the counter. "I want to talk about my divorce with someone who doesn't know me or my husband."

"An unbiased opinion?"

"Yes."

"Alright, shoot."

"You're okay with this?"

He stopped short of drinking more tea, just holding the glass in the air about an inch from his mouth. "I really don't have anything to do when I'm not working or I'm not at church. Besides, how many people can say they provided an unbiased opinion for *Constance Wells*?" He snorted.

"You know who I am?"

"Nah, but you must be important if you were dining at The Palace."

"Right," I said. "Well, then, you really are perfect. You don't know a thing about me." I could feel myself sinking further into relief as I made my way to a seat beside him.

"Daniel James," I started, "we met in college, dated for three years, and got married when I turned twenty-two. And then, nine months ago, after five years of marriage, he decided I wasn't 'The One' anymore. I just don't know where I went wrong."

"Why do you say that?"

"Because he stopped loving me. I must've been too hard to get along with or maybe I was in the way of his dream for the company, because now he's trying to build his own."

"Really? That's low."

"It is, but I don't even know why he's doing this. I mean, what does not being 'The One' even mean after eight years together?"

"I don't know, honestly."

"He didn't even speak to me during the entire divorce process. All our communication was filtered through a lawyer!" I tried to control my anger, but I could feel it swelling inside me. I sipped my tea to stop myself from yelling.

"I think maybe you shouldn't talk about this," the kid said with wide eyes.

I nodded, wiping a drop of tea from my mouth. "This was a mistake, bringing you in here to talk."

"Why?"

"Because I can't keep myself together and you're just a kid—a kid I don't even know."

"How have you survived the last nine months?"

"I haven't." I stood. "I've been going through the motions, day in and day out. I don't feel anything. I'm never hungry or tired. So I'm not sleeping very well. I just exist right now."

"Well, it's better than *not* existing, right?"

"I don't know." I walked to one of my living room windows and stared outside. The shimmering blue sky looked like the sun had settled in the ocean with no clouds in sight. I used to love staring out at the blue sky, daydreaming of a perfect future with Danny. "But now that's gone," I whispered. I could feel a lump forming in the back of my throat, tears burning my eyes, and memories clouding my mind. "Why didn't God save me?" I said quietly as I sank to the floor. "Why didn't He help me? Why am I facing this? Why lose my marriage, my mind, and soon my business?"

I could hear his footsteps trailing over to me before he sat beside me on the floor. When I glanced over at him, he was looking out at the blue sky too, staring at the rolling grass, the little house I had built on the property for the housekeepers, and my glistening pool.

"My mother died almost three years ago," he said in a deep voice. "About four hours before my high school graduation. She had cancer."

My tears seemed to halt at once. There wasn't any mist in his eyes, or tears rolling down his dimpled cheeks. He was just looking out the window, like he was lost in thought as he spoke.

"I loved my mom," he went on. "Just like anyone. She'd been battling cancer my entire four years of high school. It was hard; we were in mounds of debt because of her treatment. So far behind in bills, they just stopped sending them. Food was hard to come by, so you can imagine I couldn't play sports. I loved football," he shrugged, "but we couldn't afford the gear, or any of the other fees for the games and practices. But I also didn't have time for it anymore. By my junior year, the cancer had progressed so furiously in her stomach that it was only a matter of time."

"I'm so sorry, Joaquin."

"It's alright." He looked over at me, and the rays of the sun hit his eyes perfectly, making them glow like embers in the deepness of night. "I wanted to be like you. Angry that God didn't heal my mother. Angry that He took her from me. But my mother read me a passage from the Bible about three days before she died."

"What was it?" I was eager to hear anything that would bring my faith back.

"Ecclesiastes the third chapter, the first verse through the fifteenth verse. It talks about a time, or a *season*, for everything."

I nodded.

"Solomon didn't leave out a season for crying and a season for grieving. That was because he knew that no matter what, we were going to face those hard times. And no matter what, the time for laughter and dancing will come again. But my favorite verse is the fifteenth verse. The one about the things that will happen has already happened."

I nodded, watching him speak proudly, as if he wasn't even talking about his mother who'd passed away. Sure, he had nearly three years of grieving under his belt now, but losing a mother, losing a loved one in general, is not something people are strong about so soon.

"It connects to that one scripture in Jeremiah, where God tells Jeremiah that He knew him before He formed him in his mother's womb." He offered a tiny smile. "God had already put these seasons in place before I was even born, which means, He's already placed good in my life too. I just had to be strong enough to get to the good stuff. But I learned that it was okay to be weak, because God's strength is perfect when we're weak."

"So, it's okay that your mom passed away because it was predestined?"

He shook his head. "It's okay to lose things because your *return* is also predestined. We forget that sorrow is a currency in our faith. Every tear, every misfortune, every bad thing that comes our way, God promises restoration to the Believer in the Book of Joel."

"Sorrows are a currency," I said slowly.

"They are. And every time you trade in your sorrows—joy, comfort, restoration, and strength are returned."

"I've never heard it said like that before."

He leaned back and scratched his head. "Sometimes hearing things a little differently can restart your engines."

"I guess so."

"Well," he began to stand, and I followed, "I better get going now."

"I thought you said you could stay all day?" I smirked.

He chuckled. "If you're just dying for me to stay, Constance, then I'll stay."

For the first time in a long time, I felt my lips curl into a real smile, not a forced one, or just something to hide the pain. It felt even more genuine than the laugh Keesha gave me today.

"Thanks for hearing me out, Joaquin."

"No problem." He leaned over and set the keys to the Rolls Royce on the counter.

"You sure you don't want the car?"

"Yeah. I don't really need it."

"Well, let me at least pay you for everything."

He waved me off. "Nah, don't sweat it."

"You sure?"

He dropped his hands into his pockets and gave me a nod before seeing himself out.

4

Constance

"Vivian," I called as I flipped through a stack of papers.

A small woman who always wore long necklaces and ballet flats walked into my office. "Yes, Ms. Wells?"

"I need you to do me two favors."

"Of course." She tucked her skirt and sat, pulling a pen from behind her ear, and a pad of sticky notes from between her heavy breasts. "I'm ready when you are."

"Right…" I glanced back down at the paperwork. "I need you to bring me every client of Daniel James—separated into three categories. Category one will be all the clients I've met with in the last few months and have secured business with them. Category two will be clients I've met with, secured with, and are currently working a case for them. And the last category—"

"Will be ones you haven't met with in the last nine months. Correct?"

I nodded, and she flashed me her best smile. "That's why

you're my favorite secretary," I said.

She laughed, tossing a hand at me. "Ms. Wells, I'm your only secretary."

"That's because no one is more suited for this than you."

She straightened her shoulders and lifted her chest. "Of course not."

"Now ... the second favor—and make sure you get this last name—I'm looking for a woman with the last name *Ramirez*. She died almost three years ago of stomach cancer and left behind a lot of bills."

Viv didn't speak, she listened and jotted down my every word on her sticky pad. I could tell from her rigidness; she was wondering where this had all come from.

"I'm paying off a debt I owe her. She's a friend of mine from way back," I explained.

"And you can't remember her first name?"

"A lot of things have slipped my mind lately."

"So how am I supposed to know who she is?"

"She would've died in June—late June—about three years ago, around high school graduation time. And she has a son, Joaquin Ramirez. He's a…"

Her pen stopped and she looked up at me, waiting for an answer.

"He's a valet driver at The Palace."

She didn't move.

"Write that down," I insisted.

"Isn't he the boy who—"

"If you say anything about this, Vivian, I will make sure

you can't ever get another job, not even as a prostitute. Got it?"

Her brows sat high over her big round glasses as she muttered, "Yes, ma'am."

"Good. Now go."

"Can I ask one thing?" Vivian had recovered already, clearing her throat, and speaking as if I hadn't just threatened her career. Honestly, she was never fazed by my threats. She's always kept the company's secrets, though we've never had many of them.

Initially, I was worried about my privacy when the divorce began, and she brought the papers in during a meeting. I thought she'd done it on purpose because she'd read the papers and knew what they were. But when I questioned her later, she didn't have a clue—thankfully. Viv had never read the papers. Just delivered them and moved on.

It made sense, considering the day my husband served me with papers, his secretary was not there, and her desk and his office were cleaned out. They'd done it through the night since she (and now Viv) had a key to the building.

"What is it?" I asked.

Viv grinned. "Is he at least handsome?"

"Get out, Vivian."

"Yes, Ms. Wells."

She was the only person besides Keesha who didn't cheer *against* me during the divorce. I wasn't sure why she was so loyal, but I was grateful for her.

The rest of the day was a bust. No one mentioned the incident at The Palace, but I could hear their whispers and I definitely noticed their stares as I walked through the office. The company owned an entire building of offices, but the top floor—where I worked—was the most suffocating. Probably because Danny made everyone feel equal, which was good. But the fine line between respecting people and treating an employee as they should be treated had gotten blurred in our office.

People met deadlines, people were accurate, and I was grateful. But people were also mouthy and sometimes treated me less like a boss and more like an unpopular high school teacher. Danny never got the thick of it, but I was *always* the one who saw the complaints, the eye rolls, the smack talk when I asked them to do something extra. It was like this whole office had always hated me; I just never knew it.

"Maybe I should just close the entire office. Just quit and don't come back," I muttered to myself, sitting alone in my office later that afternoon.

"Now, Ms. Wells, that's not an option. I have bills to pay," Viv said as she set a black coffee down on my desk. The smell was of poison, which was how I'd been taking my coffee recently. As black as death, as vile as sickness. The bitter strong taste chased the feelings of regret and anger and sadness away.

"No one has ever liked me here," I complained, well aware of how pathetic I sounded. I owned an incredibly successful business and I was upset that no one liked me. I know it was childish to even care, but I *did* care. Was it such a crime to *want* to be liked?

"I have always liked you," Vivian protested.

"Yeah, Viv, I know. It's just more obvious now. It feels like everyone had been tolerating me all this time for Danny's sake, and now that they're stuck with me, they're not afraid to let me have it."

"Why don't you fire them all?"

"Because that's unethical. And because I need them."

"You need a *vacation*," she said as she opened a folder and set it in front of me.

"What's this?" I reached for my glasses.

"This is category one; all the clients in this folder haven't made any qualms about the change in business personnel. But these accounts highlighted in red," she pointed. "They're all missing accounting information."

"How is that possible?"

She shrugged. "I went into the system and there's nothing there."

"Ok … Wait … were there any other accounts like these in the other categories?"

Her face became glum as she placed the other two folders atop the first one. When she opened the folder labeled category two, I gasped. Every single client that we were working with was highlighted in red and asterisked.

"What's the asterisk for?" I asked, not quite sure I wanted to hear the answer.

"It means they stopped payment. The retainer fee hasn't been received in the last three months."

I covered my face. Something painful and dark cracked open in my chest; I took a deep breath to clear it out and calm down. "Are you serious?"

"It gets worse."

I was positive that wasn't possible.

"Worse than clients I've already worked with backing out?" I said incredulously.

She nodded. "Category three, clients you haven't reached out to yet." She opened the folder, and it was blank.

"There's not a single client in our updated system, but I went down two floors, and there's a guy down there who I've had lunch with a few times. He was able to find the original files saved or backlogged before the changes three weeks ago."

"Three weeks ago." I stood and snatched my glasses off. "They've been *removed* from our system."

"Yes, the rest of Daniel's clientele no longer exists within our system."

"He's taking everything from me."

"I did one more thing; pulled up some of the accounting files." She set down another folder, but I didn't look at it right away. I didn't know if it could take anymore.

"You've got three more payments from two of Daniel's accounts before you'll have lost nearly half the company in big business. If this goes on, your salary alone will crumble the company in two months' time."

Slowly, I reached for my chair and sat down. "You're kidding me."

"I wish I was. But I crunched some numbers and if we—

"

"He won..." I whispered shakily. "He's taken my company from me. He's taken my money, and our marriage... I have nothing." I placed a hand on my head, and thought for a moment, "What am I going to do?"

"Fool them," Vivian said darkly.

"What?"

"Fool your investors by selling all your stock back. They'll think you're selling it back in an angry fit because of your ex-husband's fiancée. You'll have enough money to cover yourself for a while since you know they're going to buy that stock up."

"Why would anyone invest in our company if they don't like me?"

"Because they're thinking they're going to crowd you out before you get over your angry fit. You take that money from the investors, and you start over. Do it all by yourself."

"Viv—"

"I mean start with me of course," she smiled, "it's *our* only way out."

"Doing this would mean the debt and the problems incurred won't be on me."

"Exactly, you'll no longer be a stakeholder, and I can quietly get you and me off the books through my friend."

"Isn't he in accounting? Won't he know what you're doing?"

"He's not actually in accounting," her smile stretched into a grimace, "he hacked the accounting software to get in. He's a tech guy."

I raised a hand and waved it. "I don't even want to know if I should be angry or not." I lowered my hand to my armrest and looked around. For five years, my ex-husband and I built this company. Letting it fall seemed horrible and wrong. But I had no choice. If I didn't get out before the ship sank, I'd drown with it. My name was already tarnished, so stepping out now wouldn't make me look any worse than I already did.

I sat there for a moment in silence, enjoying my privacy and what little pride I had left for just a little longer. Then I swallowed that pride and tried to think of a plan.

Getting out was my only option despite how badly it hurt. I wanted to make this company work despite losing Daniel. Surrendering meant he'd won, and that he'd taken everything from me. The only thing that gives me solace is that he won't take it publicly.

"Alright, Viv, here's what I want to happen." I sat forward in my chair, a new anger bubbling in my chest. "I want you to get my name, your name, and that tech guy off the books by Friday, close of business." Viv started furiously jotting things down again. "Saturday night, I'm going back to The Palace to meet with the kid I told you about."

She paused. "Joaquin Ramirez?"

"Yes."

"Why?"

"To make it look like I'm starting a new business endeavor. I'll take the files and present to him that I've paid his mother's debt. But I need a back table, in private."

"I'll make the reservation, but what's the point?" Her brow

was arched above her glasses.

I said, "You said investors will think I'm just angry, right? So, let's make them think I actually want out. They'll buy me out to *keep* me out, like you said, thinking that I'm copying my ex-husband and starting a new business with the kid."

"I see." She nodded slowly, thinking it over. "They'll crowd you out so quick, bid even higher on your stock."

"Exactly. But put shares up for sale three hours before my date. No one checks the stock on Saturday because the market is closed. But having it up there before the date makes it look more official."

She took a breath, unsure how to phrase her next words. I braced myself.

"You know you'll be a laughingstock, right?"

"This was *your* idea." I sat back in my chair, feeling a little devious.

"My idea was to just sell the shares, not do all *this*."

"I need it to be believable. A little extra drama and the prices will go up."

"Alright, I'll set everything up for you. Do you want me to get in contact with Ramirez?"

"Yes, get him a suit for the dinner as well. And make sure you cover his day's wages."

"Of course." She stood, setting the final folder on my desk. "I found her, so you can take a look at that information yourself. If you want."

"Thanks. And—Vivian?"

She turned, slipping a finger to her lips. "Not a word," she mocked.

I laughed, grateful for how much I could trust this woman. "Thank you."

5

Joaquín

Holding the leg of the chair, I twisted the Allen wrench until the small screw tightened. "There," I said to myself, "that should hold up for a while." Flipping the chair over, I shook it a little to make sure it was sturdy. Our dining set was falling apart, but thankfully, I've gotten pretty handy since Mom got sick. When the illness first started, Dad was working, so I was left to take care of Mom and the house. Needless to say, I learned a few things.

"Keem!"

"Yeah?" I called.

"There's a woman here for you," Shelley called from the front door. I didn't know why she hung around the house when Dad wasn't home, or why Dad let her start living with us two months ago. We'd been a Believing family until Shelley came along. I didn't dislike her, she's actually really cool. But after eight years of sobriety, my dad went back to drinking, and now he and Shelley were always going at it—whether I'm home or not.

Initially, I was a little taken aback by how quickly my dad got over my mother. Then, I was happy for him because he'd finally gotten himself together. He'd stopped the hurt and he'd moved on. I was so happy to see him come alive again, I didn't even care that he'd found another woman. I was just glad to have my pops back. But when Shelley started coming around more, I changed my mind again. I just can't figure out how my father moved on from my mother to a woman like this. A woman who's nothing like Mom.

Shelley came down the hall in my dad's t-shirt and sweatpants. Her blonde hair was tied back as she ate my leftovers. I stared at the container of food in her hands, trying to decide if I wanted to react or not. I chose to ignore her thievery when she got my attention.

"Keem," she snapped, "the door?"

"Right."

I slipped by her down the hall and pushed open the screen door. There was a woman standing on the porch. She had tanned skin and a big afro. She was kind of cute, but I was more interested in the envelope in her hand. She wore leather gloves that looked expensive, I couldn't stop flicking my gaze between the letter and her covered hand, staring at the material, admiring the way it curved with the movements of her hand. Her gloves made me give her a second glance. Her clothes looked pricey; I'd never seen a *pencil skirt* look so expensive.

"You must be Joaquin Ramirez?" She worded it like a question.

"Who's asking?" I nodded.

"I'm Vivian Balla, secretary of Constance Wells."

"Constance?"

"Yes, you know her?"

"Well…" I glanced off, unsure how well I knew Constance, or how much Constance would be alright with me telling what I knew of her. "I've seen her at my job before."

"Ah," the woman nodded, "well I actually have a bit of information for you. Do you mind if I come in?"

I glanced back at the door, slapping a hand to my neck. If I took her inside, my dad's girlfriend would yap to the entire neighborhood about whatever this woman has to say. But if we walk, people will see us and ask me about this lady. But just because they asked doesn't mean I have to answer. Then again, walking with a lady dressed this nicely ran the risk of being robbed or at least roughed up if anyone thought I was making bank with this fancy woman. Especially since this would be the second time in one week that I went off with a random rich woman.

Letting out an exhausted sigh, I asked, "Do you mind walking? My dad's girlfriend is a little…"

"No worries," she laughed, "we can take my car for a ride."

We got into her white Mercedes, and she drove us to a hamburger joint. She took us through the drive thru, and then we parked around back where no one could see us.

"Why are we parked back here?" I asked as I munched on fries.

"Because I actually need your help with something."

I frowned. "With what?"

"Constance needs you to go on a date with her."

"What?" I almost sucked down an extra long fry.

The woman ignored my choking. "Her business is failing, and she's trying to get out before everything falls on her. So, having dinner with you will be a coverup story for her."

"Seriously?" I didn't want to admit how cool it sounded to be part of something like this, but I also couldn't avoid the nervous feeling I was getting. "Why me? And what happens if I don't do this?"

"Constance has a good reason for seeing you again," she explained. "But I'll let her tell you that if you agree to this dinner."

"And if I don't?"

"Then I'm sure Constance would come see you regardless."

I rolled my eyes. From what I'd learned about that woman, I'd say it was just like her to march up to my front porch and drag me out to dinner whether I wanted to go or not. But being seen with Constance at *work* was one thing, I couldn't take another rich woman coming into my *neighborhood* looking for me.

"Fine," I shrugged, "I'll go to dinner."

"Perfect."

"This won't get me in trouble with the police, right? Because we're in debt and I don't think we can afford bail."

"No, you'll be perfectly fine. Besides," she grabbed her

purse and pulled out the envelope from before, "here's a day's wages for dinner on Saturday night at eight. A car will be here to pick you up at six-thirty. You'll be taken to Constance's place to meet up with her, and a driver will take you both to The Palace."

I was counting the money as she talked, "There's a lot more than a day's wages in here."

"Constance also included money for a suit. She needs you to look the part on Saturday. So, Friday morning, a car will be here to take you to a fitting."

"Hold on," I shook my head, "I've got to go get a suit on Friday and go to dinner Saturday night?"

"Yes. I included Friday's wages in case you'd need to take off work for the fitting."

"Yeah, I'll have to take a half-day Friday," I said as I closed the envelope. "All this for one day." I sighed, suddenly feeling exhausted.

"Sorry," Vivian apologized, she'd told me her pretty name before ordering the food. I glanced over at her as she offered a weak smile. "Just bear with us."

"I mean, what else can I do?" I shrugged.

"She'll be so pleased that you agreed."

"One more thing," I stopped her. "Can you meet me at a different location? I just don't want my neighborhood asking around."

"Of course." Vivian pulled a pen and pad from her purse and offered it to me. "Jot down the location and I'll arrange for the driver to come get you there."

"Thanks," I said as I wrote down my church's address. It's usually closed on Friday and Saturday, so it'll be fine to get picked up from there. The side door is always open, but it only leads to the sanctuary, so I'd change in there.

"Here," I passed back the pad, "how'd you find me anyway?"

She smiled. "I've got my ways."

^_^

Saturday night came quickly. Before I knew it, I was dressed in the most expensive clothes I'd ever worn. A crimson red velvet suit with black leather lapels. My shirt beneath was a silky material that the seamstress said would keep me cool. I didn't wear a tie; instead, I left the first three buttons of my shirt undone—as the seamstress insisted. The entire suit was customized to fit me perfectly, and my black shoes with red bottoms were the icing on the cake. My feet felt like heaven as I walked out the church and got into the car waiting for me.

The seats were comfortable, and the driver had greeted me with a head nod, murmuring a greeting. I only nodded since I couldn't hear him through the partition. As we drove down the highway, I could feel myself getting more and more nervous. I really didn't understand exactly how going to dinner with me would get Constance out of her failing business, but I didn't want to pass up an opportunity to eat at The Palace. Mr. Adams didn't let us eat the food. He always said it was only for the guests. So, over the past few months I've been working there, I've never tasted a single dish.

Our car pulled up to Constance's house, and the driver got out to open my door. I'd taken the liberty of buying Constance some flowers as a thanks for choosing me to help her with this crazy endeavor. My mind couldn't stop wondering about her reasons behind all this, but Vivian assured me that Constance would tell me tonight.

I walked up to the door and rang the doorbell. My hands were soaked with sweat as I gripped the bundle of blood red roses. I tried to stay calm, but I suddenly had a strike of fear chip at my heart when I thought I forgot to put deodorant on. I sighed the thought away when I remembered packing it in a zip pocket on my duffle bag and using it. I only remembered using it because I dropped it in the sanctuary, and it made a white streak on the carpet that I had to clean up.

The door opened, and a woman stood there with a sucker in her mouth. Brown skin like Constance, and tight coils of hair, the woman smirked around her lollipop.

"I see why Constance picked you," she remarked.

"Uh," I let out a really nervous sigh and she waved a hand, smacking on her sucker, "Don't be nervous," she told me. "Come on in." She reached out and grabbed my arm. "You smell good, you look good, and you got her flowers? You like my girl Constance, huh?"

"What? No," I staggered, "I got her these because I thought I should. Like a thank-you, or something." Now I felt dumb for getting the flowers and I was ready to throw them out the window, take my suit off, and race down the driveway back home. But the woman holding my arm kept me grounded so I couldn't run.

"Y'all would be cute together," she teased.

My only reaction was a dry swallow as we waited in the foyer.

"Let me go get her." The lady patted my arm and tiptoed around the corner. "Connie! There's an absolute honeysuckle down here waiting on you. And if you don't come get this honeysuckle, *I* will!"

"Keesha!" I heard Constance yelling from somewhere in her mansion.

Keesha laughed as she rounded the corner. Long legs stretched beneath her short-shorts, reaching me before she did. "Here she comes." Keesha grinned. "So, what's your name?"

"*Me llamo,*" I paused, "sorry. I'm nervous." I shook my head.

"Dang, your default when you're nervous is to *speak Spanish*?" She said this like I'd spoken an alien language.

"It's my first language," I admitted.

"Ooh!" Her grin stretched even wider, and she nearly swallowed that sucker whole. "Constance, you better come get him!"

"My name's Joaquin Ramirez."

She placed a hand on her hip and bit into her sucker with a crunch. "And mine is Keesha. So you're half Spanish?"

"Half Mexican." I nodded, "My mom was Black American, and my Dad's Mexican."

"*Was?*" She paused. "Has your mom passed?"

"Yes. In a few months, she'll have passed three years... ago." I got distracted as Constance's footsteps clicked out before she came around the corner. Just when I thought I'd have to swallow the awkward emotional reaction to telling a stranger about my mother, my mind was wiped clean and all I could think about was how beautiful Constance looked. She was a welcome distraction.

"Her hips," I whispered, but Keesha's cackling beside me told me it *wasn't* a whisper.

I didn't care. I couldn't even look away.

I'd seen Constance in a dress suit—she was nice looking. The next day she was in a big bathrobe, and no makeup. She was still nice looking. But nothing could've prepared me for this.

The way her round hips swayed with every step as her black dress clung to her in ways that made me wonder who would ever give her up. She had a rack, but I wasn't surprised since I'd gotten a few looks at her in that corset. But her sweetheart neckline, exposing her smooth chocolate skin, made my heart race incredibly fast. Loose curls were pinned back, with a few hanging loose over her bare shoulders.

"Are those for me?" Her voice was sweeter than I'd ever heard it. Bright red lips and long fluffy lashes, I couldn't formulate words, so I just shoved the flowers at her. "Goodness," she replied as she took them. "You didn't have to do this, Joaquin."

"I-I-I..." I stopped talking and swallowed. "I just thought it'd be nice."

"Well, thank you." She smiled gently. "I'll take these and place them in water before we leave."

I watched her trail off when I felt a fiery swack to my arm.

"She looks good, doesn't she?" Keesha was cheesing.

"Ye-Yeah."

"You guys are going to drive the place crazy today," she said with a confident smile.

"No," I shook my head, "she's going to drive *me* crazy."

"Does she look that good to you?"

"I've never seen someone look like her before."

Keesha gave me a coy smile before pulling her eyes back to the foyer entrance where Constance came through. I almost had another heart attack as she approached again. Even if it was only one night, I don't think I'd ever get used to how beautiful she looked.

"Are you ready?" she asked as she grabbed my arm.

"Mmhmm," I nodded.

"Alright, Keesha, I'll be back later tonight."

"Wait," she waved as she pulled out her phone, "let me get a picture."

"This isn't prom night," Constance complained.

"So what?" Keesha's voice was high pitched now. "I still wanna get a flick of my best friend looking good with her date, who is fine. How old are you?" Keesha asked, snapping a picture of us.

"I'll be twenty-one soon."

"Ooh, you got a youngin'!"

"Keesha, please go away." Constance squeezed my arm a

little tighter.

Just then, the car honked outside, and I heard Constance exhale.

"We have to go," she told Keesha. "I'll see you tonight."

In the car, Constance sat with her legs crossed. I couldn't help but sneak glances at her perfectly smooth thighs that were on display from the split in her dress. *I've never seen a woman like this before,* I thought. Constance was an adult—nothing like the ladies my age at all. My eyes traced her in the evening light as she scrolled through her phone. Long nude nails, small hands, a full chest, and pouty lips made Constance a woman I could only dream of getting to know. She looked like a celebrity; it was hard to believe I was about to go on a date with her.

"Ok," she said abruptly. She looked up from her phone and caught me staring, even though I tried to look off. Mercifully, she didn't shame me, she just kept talking. "So, what did my secretary tell you?"

"She said you needed me to help you get out of your failing business."

One of her brows jutted upward, but she only nodded before she added, "Right. Tonight, I need you to act the part of an interested party."

"What exactly am I interested in?"

Her eyes widened, and then she glanced off. I swear the question made her blush, but her stern voice said otherwise. "You're interested in business."

"Only?"

"Mostly..." She looked back at me, her expression flat. "Being interested in anything more than business will just stir the pot, but we want that—to *some* degree. So, a little flirting here and there is fine. But it mostly counts when we step out the car."

A little flirting, I thought excitedly. More excitedly than I should have. I couldn't help myself.

"Keem, are you listening?"

"Yeah," I paused, "when'd you start calling me *Keem*?"

"Oh," she clasped her hands together, "I thought, at least for tonight, it'd be a good idea to use a nickname to make it seem more personal."

"So, you want me to call you Connie, then?"

She nodded. "That's fine."

A shallow silence fell over us.

I didn't know what to say, but Connie didn't let the silence linger anyway. She started again, explaining how the night needed to go.

"When we arrive, the driver will open your door. You step out and open my door for me. Don't let the driver do it."

"And then we walk inside. Together. Right?"

"Yes. Get inside, get seated. We'll get some drinks and then we'll do some business discussions, or whatever."

"Vivian mentioned you wanted to give me something."

"I do, that'll be the business we discuss. I'd tell you now, but I want to wait because I need your raw and honest reaction."

"Alright, this sounds easy."

"Good," she said. "Because we're almost there, and we've got to make this look good."

6

Constance

Our car pulled into the valet parking lot. There was an older man working as one of the valet attendants; when I glanced over at Joaquin, he was smiling like he recognized the man. It could've been anyone that night who'd stopped me from starting an all-out brawl here, so why him? This valet kid, with nothing but the world in his eyes, is the one sitting beside me.

I sighed, but he spoke before I did.

"Are you ready?"

"Uh, yeah."

Joaquin took a breath as the driver spoke to the valet attendant. When he got out and came around to open the door, I could hear the laughter spilling from The Palace, and the questions calling from The Palace's entrance. There were always paparazzi here, or journalists trying to get the next big story. Celebrities, athletes, and all kinds of high-class people visited The Palace.

I was counting on that.

High class people loved gossip more than anyone in the world because, most of the time, us 'rich folk' were 'poor folk' once who enjoyed fan-girling over celebrities too. Becoming a celebrity or becoming important didn't remove that kid inside who longed to meet their favorite actor, singer, athlete, whatever. But none of that mattered now. All I needed was for the gossip about Constance Wells stepping out with her new fling/business partner to take over the media.

Keem stepped out of the car. There was an audible gasp from the crowd of journalists and flashing cameras. I watched him move around the car, drinking in this moment. My confidence swelled with every flash of photography. The sound of the chattering journalists was like music to my ears. They were eating Joaquin up, and the real show hadn't even begun. It helped that Keem was handsome, of course, he almost looked like he belonged here—and he was so comfortable in front of the crowd. Keem had been a valet attendant at The Palace so he was used to the cameras and journalists. I thought being on the opposite side of things would make him nervous, but he seemed at ease as he opened the door for me.

I put one leg out. Then the other. The cameras flashed in anticipation. With a calming breath, I grabbed Keem's hand and stepped out of the car. Gasps and oohs roared and it sounded like the cameras would never stop clicking.

For a second, we both stood there. Staring at each other. Not really sure what to say or do next.

"Keem? Is that you?" the older valet attendant called,

interrupting our moment.

Casually, Joaquin found my waist and held me by it as the valet attendant came over to us. I tried not to stare at him in awe. It was like the nervous kid from the car had totally disappeared. This was the man who would turn everything around for me. I knew it in my soul.

"Kenny," Joaquin said as he turned and closed the car door. "How are you?"

"What are you doing here, man?" The two slapped hands, pulling each other into an embrace before Joaquin found my waist again. I hadn't been pulled close to someone in months and having his hands around me made me feel more flustered than I could almost bear. "I'm here for business," Keem said, then he looked at me and winked. "And for a little something else." He laughed with Kenny, and causally corrected himself since I'd said nothing in response. "Well, hopefully a little something else," he added as Kenny cackled loudly.

"Keem, we should go inside," I said quietly, hoping he didn't hear the nerves making my voice shake. This anxiety was so unlike me, but I couldn't help it. I didn't even know why I was suddenly flustered. Was it the excitement of the moment? The fact that everything seemed to be working out according to plan—when everything had seemed so off-course last few months? Was it the paparazzi? I'd been surrounded by them plenty of times, but for once this attention was good for me, and I wasn't quite used to that again.

Or was it Keem...

I didn't even want to think about that possibility or what

it meant for me and my weird emotions. So I took a breath and repeated myself while Keem and Kenny continued their banter.

"We should go inside."

There was a pleading note in my voice, which caught his full attention, and when his eyes landed on me, I felt my breath trying to escape in fear. I was so nervous with this kid. I was afraid my legs wouldn't move if Joaquin talked to Kenny for any longer.

"Well, listen, Kenny," Keem said, his grip on my waist pulling me even closer.

I can't breathe.

"My date is ready to eat. We can catch up later."

"Man, I heard you'd called off work, but I didn't know it was for this." Kenny looked at me like he was hungry. I half expected him to bark at me. Keem must have noticed the look because he leaned closer to me and began guiding me away. His arm was still around my waist, but now it felt different. No longer flirtatious, but… possessive.

I was two seconds from fainting.

It's a real shame what divorce does to a woman. It eats at you from the inside out, devouring all the soft parts first. The parts that tell you you're beautiful and valued and worth something. They leave you a hollowed skeleton, a shadow of the woman you used to be. And all that's left when it's over is this creature you hardly recognize. A woman who is so deeply convinced that she is *not* loved and she is *not* valued and she is *not* worth a penny, that she falls for a guy because he did nothing more than hold her hand and say nice things to her.

As I looked at Keem, watching him play the hero and lead me away from Kenny, I wondered if he knew who I was. If he saw the hollow skeleton or if the flashing cameras were too bright for him to see past.

He smiled as Kenny said goodbye. "You owe me for covering for you, Keem."

"I gotchu," Keem said before looking down at me. "You ready, Connie?"

"Y-Yes."

We walked between the cars, Keem guiding me with his hand, and I could see the eager faces wanting a story. I could see their mouths moving but I couldn't hear them. I didn't want to. The people who will write a story about me tonight will be here again tomorrow writing a different story about someone else.

No one has ever truly cared about me, not even Danny. As we approached the steps, I couldn't shake the annoying feeling that all of this was fake. Pointless. Vain. Danny and I dined at The Palace every so often, and it never felt like this back then. But remembering the way he used to protect me from the journalists, guide me through the sea of people hungry to keep their job, not just write a story, I began to hate it all. I began to hate the lies, the smiles, the thoughts of Daniel.

I'd come back too soon. I had no idea what I was thinking. Taking a young man on a date to prove something? Who was I proving something to? What was I even proving?

"Connie," Keem's voice snapped me to reality. He was

standing on the step, extending a hand to me. I don't know how long I'd been standing there, but seeing Joaquin made the rush of dark emotions ease a little. "We can go home," he said as he walked back down the steps to me. His hands were on me again, both of them pulling me into him right in front of everyone.

"Keem," I whispered as I glanced around.

"It's me and you, Constance." His words pulled my attention from the snapping cameras. "What do you want to do?"

"I … I don't want to let it bother me," I whispered.

"If you're not ready, we can go home and come back another day."

"No." I shook my head as the crowd around us began to fade, just for that moment.

Joaquin had some kind of power, I think. The way he held me, focused on me, considered me. It was new, despite being married for five years. Things like being held, or focused on didn't happen very often between Danny and me. We were always working, and by the time we got home, we were catty and exhausted, aggravated and wanted to be alone most of the time… at least Danny did. I don't remember when the smiling stopped, the pool dates stopped. But that didn't matter now, and it would never matter again.

"I want to do this," I said. "I have to."

"Alright." His hand slipped from my waist and took my own hand in his. "Then we'll take it slow."

I nodded as he turned and guided me up the stairs and into

The Palace. The red doors opened, and golden light poured over us. Glistening gold tiles, and white walls that reached a blue dome painted with baby cupids shooting golden arrows welcomed us. A woman in black pants and a vest waved us to her booth.

"Reservation, please?" she said in French.

"Ramirez for two," Joaquin replied in French.

I was floored, but only watched as the woman scrolled her screen and nodded.

"A table for two, back round table, leather seats. Correct?"

"*Oui*," Joaquin said. His accent sounded real, like French was his first language.

"Perfect. Follow me," the attendant said.

Joaquin and I walked through the restaurant, hand in hand. All eyes were on us, ogling, and gasping at us. Briefly, I enjoyed it. I felt like I was regaining a little of what I lost earlier this week when I found out my ex had a fiancée. Though, I'm sure most people thought I looked stunning while simultaneously thinking I was a fool for being with a kid, let alone the *valet* kid. At the very least, Joaquin looked handsome tonight… very handsome.

His clothes fit like they were threaded for him, not tailored. His jacket clung to his physique, easing from his broad shoulders to taper into his slim waist. The silk shirt underneath pulled the entire outfit together, making him look less like the valet kid, and more like a kid born with a silver spoon in his mouth. But ultimately, it was Joaquin's confidence as we walked through the restaurant that made me weak in the knees.

This was the second time he seemed different. The first was when I saw him outside of valet work; he looked totally different. Tonight, Joaquin had showed me a new side of himself, and I kind of liked it.

"Here you are. I'll have a waiter over soon," the attendant said.

"*Merci*," Joaquin replied in French again.

When the attendant was gone, and we were seated, I tapped the table. "What was that?"

"What?" He blinked at me over the rim of his water glass, slipping slowly. Each table was always preset with water and bread and butter. He was clearly nervous because his sip turned into a gulp, and a gulp turned into an empty glass.

"Why'd you just drink all your water?"

"I'm hot," he said shakily.

I sighed. "You did good, Joaquin."

His shoulders dropped. "Really? Because I was so nervous."

"I can tell now," I nodded at his glass, "but I couldn't then."

He laughed, and he seemed more comfortable now.

"Thanks for that out there, helping me inside."

Keem shifted with a shrug. "You looked nervous, and I didn't have a clue what to do."

"So you grabbed me by the waist, tugged me into you, made me make eye contact with you, and then you tell me everything's alright?"

"It worked, right?"

I could've protested, but I didn't because it *had* worked. Joaquin had gotten my feet moving again and even though I was feeling embarrassed, I still made it inside.

"I'm sorry if it made you uncomfortable, I was just trying to get your attention. You were looking all around, and when you stopped on the stairs, you were heaving like you were about to have a panic attack."

"How did you know what to do to get me to focus?"

"I didn't," he admitted. "The waist thing might've been too much." He surrendered a shy smile. "But I didn't know if getting your attention would work the way it did with my mother. She'd have these fits sometimes, and I'd grab her shoulders, make her keep eye contact and breathe until she was better. Sometimes looking at something else takes your mind off your situation."

"I guess so." My eyes dropped to the table as I thought about Joaquin's mother. I wish I could've met her, or that she could be here to see how well he turned out.

"Keem, listen—"

"Good evening," the waiter interrupted, setting down two menus. "Can I start you off with drinks? I recommend our blistering red wine. It was aged for twelve years and has a hint of raspberry in it."

"No, thank you," I waved. "I'd just like a tonic water."

He nodded.

"Can I have a black coffee?"

I raised a brow, and Joaquin smirked. "I'd like it strong too."

"Of course, sir. I'll be right back with your drinks."

As the waiter walked away, Keem's smirk didn't leave.

"Why are you smiling like that?"

"Because I've always heard about how good the coffee is here, but I've never had it before."

"Really?"

"And ... I'm a man, of course." He shrugged. "Gotta have black coffee."

I snorted. "Slow down, Keem, you're still the valet kid."

He laughed, and for a second the atmosphere didn't feel heavy.

"Yeah, I'll be back to the valet tomorrow, but at least tonight I get to finally try some food here."

"I can't believe you've seriously never had the food here."

"Nah, Adams is real strict about only patrons eating his food, so the workers aren't allowed to have any. And I couldn't afford this." He stared at the menu. He nearly broke a sweat. "A garden salad is a hundred dollars? Are you serious? I can make that in, like, five minutes or just grab a bag of mixed salad from the grocery store."

His furrowed brows and grimace made me laugh. He was so serious about the prices, but I'd truly never paid them any attention. The cheapest thing on the menu was the salad, and I always ordered the cobb, which was a little pricier now that I looked at it.

"You've got to be kidding me," he whispered.

"It's alright, Keem, I've got it tonight."

He sighed. "Alright, next time we have one of these

meeting things, we're either going to a reasonable place that I can afford, or we're going to your really nice kitchen, and I'll make you whatever you want."

"You can cook?"

"Of course." He sat back proudly. "I'm better than everyone in here. I didn't get hired in the kitchen because I didn't have the experience. Although, I think Mr. Adams just doesn't like me because of my dad. They were good friends, but a lot of things happened between them, and I barely got the valet gig."

"I had no clue." I took a sip of water.

"Madam, sir, your drinks," the waiter spoke French again and Keem nodded along. "I'll give you a few more moments with the menu, and then I'll take your orders."

We nodded, but when the waiter was gone, Keem snapped to me, "Why didn't he just take our orders now?"

I laughed. "The longer the wait, the better. I guess."

"I'm hungry," he said as he picked up his menu. He frowned. "Who wanna wait to eat?" His complaints were hilarious, but I couldn't forget why I'd asked him here in the first place.

As I waited for the right moment to bring up his mother, I could hear him muttering things from the menu to himself.

"You speak French pretty well," I said.

"Of course," he chuckled without taking his gaze from the menu. "Mr. Adams is French, The Palace is French, and if you work here you've got to speak some kind of French."

"You're kidding, right? He made you learn French?"

"Yeah, the basics. But I picked up on it quickly since it's my fourth language."

"*Fourth?*"

He nodded, finally lowering his menu. "I speak Spanish, English, Portuguese, and now French."

"Why do you know so many languages?"

A light blush tinted his cheeks in the dim light. "I love cooking all kinds of food, so I ended up falling in love with languages. I had to cook a lot for my mother when she was sick, and so I came across recipes and words I didn't understand and started learning them, except Portuguese." He fiddled with his menu. "I learned that one in school since I already knew Spanish and English. But I'm learning Italian and Japanese right now."

"What a funny thing to fall in love with."

"Maybe." He reached for his coffee cup. "What about you, Constance? What have you fallen in love with?"

"Do you really have to ask?" I sat back with my arms folded.

He tapped the table with his knuckles before sliding forward in his seat and resting his arms on the table. His narrowed gaze was on me now. "No, Constance, not *who* have you fallen in love with. *What* have you fallen in love with? People aren't the only things we love."

"Y-You're right," I stammered. "I guess I'd forgotten that."

"It's alright." He sat back. "You can fall in love again. Whether it be with a person or a favorite food, or a hobby. It'll happen."

His words of confidence struck a chord in me, and I reached for his hand. I think it shocked him, because he retracted into himself before glancing at our hands and then at me.

"You're very kind, Joaquin. And in a week, you've helped me more than you know. I just wanted to try and repay that." I dug through my purse and pulled out a folded sheet of paper and handed it to him.

Slowly, he took it and opened it.

His breath hitched and he covered his mouth. Tears began to form, and the paper began to tremble in his hands.

"Barb Anne Lee Ramirez left behind a debt of four hundred and fifty thousand dollars and twenty-six cents. So far, Enrique Ramirez and his son Joaquin Ramirez have paid off a total of fifty-eight thousand, four hundred and twenty-seven dollars and twenty-six cents over the past few years." I paused as his tears began to fall rapidly, and he tried to hold it all in. "You guys were paying a little more than twenty-four hundred dollars a month in medical bills and would be paying that for the next thirteen and a half years."

"Why?" He hiccupped. "Why would you pay that? We still owed almost four hundred thousand dollars... I just don't understand."

"Because you're a kid." I reached for his trembling hand again, and this time, he took my hand and held it tightly. "You're working so hard to make ends meet. I just couldn't sit by and let you struggle like that. Now when I knew I could help and that you deserved it."

"I'm scared," he whispered. "What do I do? How do I thank you?"

I waved a dismissive hand. "Joaquin, you've done enough for me. You helped me begin to trust God again. That's priceless help. So, really, this is my own thank you."

7

Joaquín

Revolvers

"Dad—"

"Where were you all night?" My father was sitting at the table, in the chair I'd fixed, reading a newspaper. I hadn't seen him all night or morning since I got in late after dinner with Connie and headed to church this morning. My father stopped going to church a while ago, but I've sent up many prayers on his behalf.

"I went out with a ... a friend."

"Shelley told me some rich-looking woman pulled up in some fancy car and took you out. What are you doing with people like that?"

Break-ins happened a lot in my neighborhood. Desperate people needing money, food, or something to sell for money. Dad and I had our house broken into twice in one month earlier this year, and then again, a little later. The first and second time we weren't home, and they took our toaster and a good deal of money. The third break-in I was home for, and I chased the guy all the way down the street until he ran into traffic. He wasn't hit by a car (unfortunately), but he did get away from me. Needless to say, because of these run-ins with Constance and Viv, suspicions about our house and what we've got inside are probably high right now.

"I can explain," I said as I pulled out a chair.

"Don't sit." He finally looked up from his paper. "You think this is a game, Joaquin? What are you trying to pull, bringing trouble to our front door?"

"Dad," I let go of the back of the chair, "if you'll give me a chance, I promise it's good news."

When he said nothing, I dug into my pocket and pulled out the paid invoice from Constance. Laying it on the table, I watched my dad silently take the paper and open it. It took him a minute to read. Slow methodical eyes traced over the entire paper before a crooked frown claimed his features.

"What is this?" he whispered as he glared at the paper.

"It's a paid invoice. My friend paid it for us." I beamed. "Dad, we're debt free! We finally took care of Mom! We finally—"

"Stop it!" he snapped, silencing me quickly. "How did you get this?"

"I spoke to a friend about Mom and—"

"You told our business? You're running around here making us look like a charity case!"

"No, Dad! Why are you upset with this? This is what we've

wanted—it's what we've *needed*. Why are you angry?"

"Because you're a fool! You paid off one debt and now you'll just owe another!"

"Constance isn't like that," I said in her defense. I couldn't understand my father's anger, and normally I'd just let it go, but Constance did a good thing for us, and I wasn't going to let him badmouth her for it.

My father's eyes burned through me as he squinted, his face distorted into a tight grimace. "*Constance?*" he questioned. "You mean the woman you almost lost your job over?" He slapped his hands to his hips as he moved across the room to me. "You sleeping with her, Joaquin?"

That… was a low blow.

I didn't pimp myself out for this. I didn't seduce Constance. And I didn't commit any other immodesty toward her. But that's how my father thinks. He believes nothing in this world is ever the result of kindness or compassion. Everything comes at a price. I knew he was like this before I told him the good news, I just didn't know he'd ever think I would reduce myself to such a low level. Or that Constance would either. She's a good woman. She's trying her best; if anyone dared to ignore the money and the glam, they would see her for who she truly is. The sort of woman who loves God and shares His compassion toward other people.

I cleared my throat. "No. I'm not sleeping with her, Pops."

He eyed me. "You *want* to sleep with her? You letting some rich trick from uptown pay all your bills so you can get some rich sex? Well, I'll tell you—it's all the same."

He backed away, but the air didn't clear. I could feel the seeds of bitterness growing in my chest. I'd sat by and let my father treat me poorly once Mom passed. Things got worse when he started dating Shelley. I didn't mind because he was happy, or so I thought. But this was too far, this was too much, over something that's supposed to be good news.

"Mom would be happy," I said behind him.

He froze, standing at the table. Slowly he turned to face me, his brows meeting each other to form a thick wrinkle of anger in the middle of his forehead. "What did you say?"

"I just don't understand your anger. Dad, please," I begged, "just tell me why you're so angry with me. I'll fix it and make things right."

"You can't fix it, Joaquin! You took money from a rich woman with hands all over the city. You really think that money was *free*?" He stepped closer to me again, his voice low. "The moment you decide to stop being her little *boy toy*, those fat cats are going to come through here and tear our house apart for what you owe them."

"Dad, you're wrong," I argued. "Constance isn't a *thug* or a user. She's a nice woman and she really cares—"

"You're so gullible!" he shouted, and in the sudden silence that followed, he hissed, "You'll do anything for a woman's attention, won't you, boy?" A very dark chuckle rolled from his mouth. "You even used your own mother's death. How many sympathy kisses did that get you? Did she invite you over after dinner to make you feel better?" He raised his voice, slamming his hand down on the table with a *thud!* "Did you roll out of her bed smelling like her perfume!"

"H-How dare you?" I moved before I knew it, closing the bit of space between us before I tackled my own father to the ground. We fell in a tangle of limbs, and I started shouting through my anger, "I would never do that to my own mother!"

"You didn't love her!" my father screamed. But his voice sounded different. He wasn't angry anymore, wasn't belittling me anymore. His voice ... it sounded strangled. Like he was on the verge of tears.

I froze, my hand gripping his shirt as tears sprung from his eyes. "No one could love your mother like I did," he sobbed, hanging limply in my grasp. "I swore *I* would pay off her debt. I swore *I* would take care of her forever. And you *took* that from me."

I stared at him in stunned silence. I had no idea Dad had been *attached* to that debt. In his mind, he was still taking care of Mom. In his mind, she wasn't gone until the debt was. But thanks to me...

I just permanently removed her from his life.

"I ... Pops ... I didn't know." I let go of his collar.

He fell over and wiped his eyes. Both of us just sat there on the floor, heaving tired, heavy breathes. Dad finally garnered his strength and sat up with a groan. He blinked at me, and I couldn't read the emotion on his face.

"Get out," he said through a sniffle.

"Dad, come on," I whispered. "I didn't mean it. I'm sorry."

"You've got one month to get out of here. For good." He

shoved himself to his feet. "If you're not out in a month, I'm calling the police."

I stared in shock as he left the kitchen, wondering what the heck had just happened.

I didn't want to be home anymore, so I left to attend the second service at my church. It was still the early afternoon, but I didn't care. I just needed somewhere to go, somewhere to think, and since the sanctuary's always open, I went there.

My head in my hands, I sat quietly on a church pew, thinking over what'd happened at home. My father loved my mother, and he'd always promised to take care of her. Before she even got sick, my mother would sometimes watch their wedding tapes with a smile as my father read his vows to her from a sheet of paper. The one she always loved and said aloud with the recording was my father's vow to take care of her.

"You are the thumping in my chest," he'd said as he concluded his vows, "you are the fragility of my masculinity, and I will always protect you. I will always take care of you because you are part of me."

My mother had explained once that my father's words were so comforting because they'd been through a lot in their relationship, but she also knew his words were straight from his heart. Protecting your masculinity—your right to call yourself a man—caring for your heart, only a fool would choose not to do those things for the woman he loved.

My father valued my mother, and she loved him for it.

"This is all part of the plan."

I looked up, and He was sitting there beside me. A book of hymns was open on the pew between us as He turned a fan back and forth in His hand.

"Am I…"

"Seeing things?" He looked up from the fan with a smile. "No, I'm here, Joaquin. I heard your prayers, and I could hear your heart breaking in confusion, and I was allowed to come visit you."

I stared. Jesus was sitting beside me. In all His glory and splendor—and yet, He was the calmest, coolest person I knew in that moment. No fancy trumpets or angels floating around. Just a beautiful man. My Father.

I blinked, watching Him examine the church fan. He seemed extremely interested in it. That's when I realized the fan had His face printed on it. He held it up beside His own face, producing a smile that could make you weep with joy.

"My people have always tried to capture My image." He lowered the fan. "But if they knew they already bore My image, it would change every one of them. There is nothing to capture or try to present. I am in them, and they are in Me."

That was true…

The picture on the fan didn't matter. The color of His skin didn't matter. The texture of His hair didn't matter. He would always be Jesus, no matter how we pictured Him in our heads. The only fact that matters is that He was human. God made flesh. And because He was made flesh, He can identify with our struggles. He can understand us and our pain because He felt it Himself when He took all our sins and sickness onto His shoulders at the Cross.

But…

"Why are you telling me this?" I asked as I found my voice again.

"Because, in bearing my image, persecution comes. Even from those you least expect it. You bore my image, and shared the Word with Constance, allowing her disbelief to vanish. She may have rewarded you, but your father became your persecutor afterward."

"How?" I bunched my shoulders together. "He has no idea what I told her."

"Though he knows not what you've said, the evidence that you have touched a life sat in his hands. Every time you share the Gospel, people are affected by it, directly, and indirectly. It's the cost of the Light."

"But, my Lord," I said, turning to Him. Thick dark waves of hair poured from his head and stopped above his shoulders, and there was an innocent glow coming from Him while a powerful aura surrounded Him. Gentle, like the lamb, and powerful, like the lion. Seeing Jesus as both the lion and the lamb had never been so real until that moment. "I know that you've said what I did for Constance helped her, and indirectly touched my father, but all it did was make him angry. How is any of this part of the plan?"

He reached out and touched my shoulder, and I felt myself surrendering to His peace. "One day soon, your father will ask what you told Constance, and when he hears the Word of God, his faith will be restored. Your father needed this encounter to begin a change in him. Sometimes, Joaquin, you are only *part* of the plan, not the one the plan revolves around."

"So... this is about my father?"

"It is. Your mother's final prayer was that you and your father would stay the course, and I will honor her prayer. This family has always been a dish made for serving, and not for tossing away. As your mother touched you, and you will touch many, your father still has a work to do for My Father."

"But he's living in sin. How can you still protect him?"

Jesus nodded. "My Father reigns over the just and the unjust, and He hears and answers the prayers of the Believers. Your mother was a Believer in Me, and so are you, Joaquin. Both of you have prayed steadily for your father, and heaven has not forgotten him."

I sat back, staring ahead at the back of the wooden pew. "God is merciful."

"Surely, He is."

8

Constance

I stabbed a straw into my homemade smoothie and left the kitchen for the living room. Thick strawberry sweetness poured into my mouth as I took a sip and sat on the couch. It almost made me forget about everything going on right now.

There was a photo album open on the sofa that I tried to ignore, even though I'd been looking through it all night. Pictures from my wedding, pictures from college, even high school pictures before I met Danny. I'd changed so much because of him; I thought I owed him everything. I thought he was the reason for my success, even my good looks. And how could I not?

How many people told me I was *glowing* after I got married? As if I'd looked a hot mess until the exact moment I said, "I do." How many people told me over and over that I had a good man. Questioned what I would do without him. Told me we were perfect together.

Everyone around me gave credit for my looks, my

endeavors, and my existence to Danny. It was only natural that, eventually, I would too.

It wasn't entirely a bad thing. In a way, I was giving credit where it was due. Your spouse is supposed to make you into a better person. Elevate you. Uplift you. And despite everything that happened later, when we first got married, Danny *did* do those things.

Daniel James was the perfect man. The perfect friend, the perfect boyfriend and fiancée. He was the perfect gentleman, son, and lover. But most of all, he was the perfect husband… at least, that's what I believed.

After only three years of marriage, he began cheating on me.

For the last two years, Danny has been in love with another woman and setting up a new life for himself without me. Sometimes people fall out of love, but most of the time they can pinpoint when and why it happened along the way. But I can't. I can't tell you when Daniel stopped loving me. I'm not even sure he ever did. I'm sure now that I was not his wife, I was his project. I was someone who made him look good and helped him start a business, someone who took so much pride in elevating him that I never realized he hadn't done the same for me. Not *after* we got married. He made it look like he had with the nice house and the cars and the booming business. But that's not love. That's just money. Daniel loved what we accomplished, but he didn't love *me*.

I think that's why I can't get over him. He left me with no real explanation, no reasoning. I'm just left to grasp and wonder while he moves on with another woman.

I don't know if I was mean to him. If I wasn't a good homemaker. If I didn't make him feel like a man. Or maybe it was shallower than that. Maybe he left because I was bad at sex. Because I wasn't attractive anymore. Because I'd started making more money and didn't need him anymore.

I just didn't know. And all the questions ate away at me. What had I done to warrant a divorce?

I stared at a photo of us on our wedding day. My white flowing gown, his white tux. We looked like two chocolate angels. We looked perfect. Maybe that should've been a red flag, just how *perfect* Daniel was. Maybe I should've known that he was really a scumbag deep down inside and had spent our entire time as boyfriend and girlfriend just pretending not to be.

Maybe he got tired of pretending for me…

I sighed as I tried not to theorize why I was sitting here alone while Danny and Jada were living the life he and I were supposed to be living.

"Who would leave me for a woman like Jada?" The words were bitter on my tongue, but I *was* bitter, so they weren't so surprising. I usually didn't say things like that out loud, but I couldn't help it anymore.

I groaned loudly, squeezing my smoothie with one hand while using my other hand to toss the photo onto the small coffee table. "What is wrong with me?" I leaned back into the pillowy cushions of my sofa. "Maybe I was too arrogant or coarse. Maybe I was too headstrong during our marriage. But

... I could've changed." I could feel a lump growing in the back of my throat. "I would've changed for him if he'd just spoken up."

Before the tears could turn into rivers, my doorbell rang. I wiped at my wet cheeks before lazily strolling to the door. It was ten at night, the only person it could've been was Keesha, but I was surprised to see Vivian when I pulled open my door.

"Hey," I said, a little stunned.

"Hey, boss lady." She smiled. "Can I come in?"

"Oh." I nodded. "Sorry, of course." I waved her inside, and she followed, stopping to dry her rain boots. "So, what's up?" I asked as we went into the living room. I didn't even bother trying to clean up the photos. Vivian knew I still wasn't over Danny, there was no need to hide it.

"Are you looking at old photos?" she asked as she stood at the coffee table. Without looking away from the album, she tossed her jacket onto the lounge chair, tucked her thick curls behind her ears, and leaned closer to the pictures on the table.

"It was a bad night," I said flatly.

"Well, it's about to be a good night now. And you're going to make room for some new pictures," she teased, pushing my photos aside. She unfolded a newspaper for me and sprawled it on the table. "Have you seen this?"

"I saw Danny on the front cover. His new agency is booming."

"I'm guessing that's why all these pictures are out now." She motioned to the coffee table and the wedding photos. "You saw his success and started feeling sorry for yourself."

"Yeah..." I flopped onto the couch, refusing to look at the newspaper.

Viv nodded at my glass full of thick frothy pink liquid. "Even got a pity smoothie for yourself."

"It's not a proper pity party without a smoothie."

Vivian laughed and then held up the paper. "Ms. Boss Lady, you're going to have to look at the paper."

"No." I slurped my smoothie and frowned. It'd gotten warm.

"Fine, then you'll miss the article about your shares getting bought up for quadruple the selling price."

I choked on my smoothie, ripping it away from my lips as a strawberry chunk tried to claw its way back up my throat. Viv took the drink and patted my back. When I'd caught my breath, I waved for her to pass me the newspaper.

Daniel had set up a system for shares. He wanted everyone to have a chance at being part of the company, so the shares were done on bids. Of course, this is a normal method for selling and buying shares, especially when there aren't many to go around, however, bidding on shares for our business only happened in the *upper* ring and the *very* lower ring.

Together, Danny and I owned fifty-one percent of the shares. He had twenty-five, and I had twenty-six percent. The next twenty percent of the company was held by board members and all the important people within the company, and that's where part of the bidding was done.

Right below them was a ten percent share for our regular office workers, people like Viv who was just my assistant. The company kept nine percent of the shares in its hand, just to gamble with when we wanted to partner with a bigger organization. But that last ten percent, the lower ring, that's the second place the bidding was done, where the public fought for shares in our company.

The bidding game allowed us to make more money than we were worth, and that's really how Danny and I made it big. We played our stocks right, and God intervened with a plan that kept the company on its feet ... right until Danny and I fell apart.

With no asking prices, the market was left up to only bidding, and initially things were tight. Mercifully though, my parents gave us a lump-sum to work with. After the first big deal, we gained some interest. But it wasn't until Daniel signed a deal with a big-name cleaning company that bidding began to *skyrocket*, and money was flowing in from the big guns regularly since our stock was sparse.

"You're absolutely rich and those suckers are stuck with the bill," Viv said as I read the headlines of page two:

Owner is Squeezed Out of Race When Shares are Leaked Over the Weekend.

My face pinched into a grimace. "Of course they make it sound like I'm a total idiot."

"But who cares!" Viv exclaimed. "You just secured a ton of money. Payouts happen instantly, which you know, and by the time anyone checks on the accounting department, they'll be withering away, scrambling at how to make up for the loss."

Glancing up from the paper, I saw Viv's smiling face, and

I felt a little excitement coursing through me. Her mood was infectious. Her joy for me could not be overlooked. She's one of the few people I've had in my corner this whole time.

I let myself smile. "I won, didn't I?"

"Yes, you did!" Viv nearly shouted.

I leaned back to take it all in. "I barely escaped from that business with my life. God has been too good to me."

"He has! So get up," Viv said, grabbing my arms, "and let's give Him a praise break, girl."

She used the sound system in my living room to put on a song, my favorite version of an old praise song I used to love. I hadn't heard it in so long that my intentions of just being quietly thankful were washed away instantly and I found myself shouting all through the living room with Vivian by my side.

We danced and laughed and sang at the tops of our lungs. I waved my hands and I screamed, "THANK YOU, JESUS!" without any care or shame.

It felt good, like I'd been shocked by a thousand volts of electricity, like my faith was rejuvenated, my mind restored, all in the instant I got to my feet and began dancing and singing around the living room. For just a moment, Danny didn't matter, the company didn't matter, I didn't even matter. Just God and His overwhelming goodness was all that was on my mind.

"Whew!" Viv squealed after we finished three songs. "I haven't seen you like this in ages."

"I'm feeling like myself again right now."

"Good," she laughed as we sat on the couch, breathing

heavily and fanning ourselves.

"You know, you made headlines twice this weekend."

"I did?" I raised a brow.

She nodded as she sat forward. Pulling her purse into her lap, she placed a magazine on the table. It was a gossip magazine, one that took pictures of you illegally and wrote their own version of your story. But none of that mattered as I sat forward to stare at the magazine. I gasped as I lifted it from the table.

"This looks like something out of a fairytale," Viv's voice was quiet as she marveled at the front cover.

Keem stood on the golden carpeted steps that led into The Palace; his suit molded to the curves of his body, his hand was extended to me, one leg on the first step and the other on the ground. He was looking at me, and as I stared at his gaze in the photo, I could remember the moment with absolute clarity.

I'd gotten caught up for a moment, thinking about Danny and everything that'd happened so far. But right here, the photographer didn't catch me in a daze. He or she caught me when Keem's voice had brought me back to reality. My eyes were fixated on him, and it looked like I was the only person who mattered to him, and he was the only one who mattered to me.

"Did you read the title?" Vivian asked, almost in a whisper. "Constance Wells is Back in the Game."

I could barely pull my eyes away from our picture as Viv continued. "There are even more pictures throughout your spread. You're the middle of the magazine. The writeup is surprisingly good; of course, there's the made-up story of how you planned the whole thing with Danny and Keem the previous week so that you could show up with Joaquin this week. But," she sighed, "other than that, you were praised for finding love again and not letting Danny take everything from you."

"It'd be nice if those things were real," I said as I set the magazine down.

Viv greedily snatched it up, flipping to my center spread. She was right, there were lots of pictures of Keem and me. Pictures of him crying, us laughing and talking all throughout dinner. Even our exit from the palace was photographed. However, the last page of our spread had a full-length picture of Keem and me, and the words beside it read; **This is What Love Looks Like.**

The rest of the spread was just using our picture as reference as the writer explained that love comes in all shapes, sizes and, apparently, *ages*. I couldn't have cared less what the writer said, it was the picture they chose that interested me.

"That's a good one," Vivian said as she leaned against me, eyeing the image.

Keem and I were standing together, his eyes locked with mine, his hands pulling me close to him. His words echoed in my mind as I stared at the picture.

It's me and you, Constance. What do you want to do?

"I don't know," I whispered.

"What?" Viv sat up.

I sighed and waved her off. "I can admit; the pictures *are* nice. The writing is so-so, though."

"Isn't it always?" Viv laughed as she brushed her thick coils away. I was hoping to avoid it, but the elephant in the room was blowing through its trunk and Viv couldn't stand it any longer. "Are you going to show him?" she blurted.

"I don't know." I shrugged. "It might give him the wrong idea."

"Or give you the wrong idea," she said with a grin.

I jerked away, blinking at her, surprised at her forwardness. But she gave an explanation, "I know that was way out of my league, but tonight we're not working, and I just want you to be happy, Constance." She took my hands and patted them, a sincere look of concern on her face.

I wanted to think more about her accusations, that I felt things for Keem, but there was no point. I was still very much in love with Danny, I had no room in my heart for Keem. I appreciated him, but nothing more than that. I couldn't afford to love someone or care about the valet kid. I paid his mother's debt as my thanks, and that needed to be the end of it.

But ... it wasn't.

Looking at that picture of Keem holding me, remembering the way my heart had skipped a beat, and how secure I'd felt when he held me, I knew trouble lurked somewhere in this story. This was a drama bomb waiting to go off.

I was trying to keep a lid on it, because I barely knew the kid, and I knew my anxious broken heart was just longing to be loved again. It wasn't fair to throw my desperation off onto Keem, he was a genuinely nice kid who deserved to fall in love for *real*. His first love shouldn't be a divorcee, it should be someone else, someone more his lane.

Sighing, I peered down at my hands in Viv's, and I knew something should be done. She was rooting for me, had always been, and it would mean the world to her if I showed Keem the spread. Plus, I knew Keesha would say the same thing when she saw the spread. She'd want to discuss it with him and tell him about how nice he looked.

"How about on Wednesday, you and Keesha and Keem all come over, and we'll look over the spread together," I suggested.

Viv squeezed my hands with a smile. I wasn't sure how it'd happened, but I knew Vivian was no longer my secretary, she'd just become a friend.

"I'll get enough copies for us," she said with a warm smile.

9

Joaquín

I got Constance's phone number. Viv gave it to me when she called me and asked me to come over today. She told me she didn't want to be the middleman anymore, so Constance had my number and I had hers.

It'd only been a few days since I last saw Constance, so I wasn't too sure about seeing her again so soon. Initially, I wasn't going to go when Viv invited me. I didn't want to make my dad any angrier, but then I remembered seeing Jesus and how He said things would work out in the end, so I decided to go.

The entire walk, I wondered if this was part of God's plans too. If seeing Constance anymore would somehow continue to affect the world around me.

When I arrived, I wasn't sure what to expect. Vivian didn't tell me anything more than to simply drop by because Constance wanted to see me. Since I wasn't working today, I was able to make it. But now that I could think about it, I probably should've asked for more details.

The door sprang open to reveal Keesha grinning ear to ear. "Hey, Keem!"

"Hey, Keesha," I said as I stepped inside. The blistering sun had been beating down on me and the frigid air conditioning felt good.

"You just get finer every time I see you." She winked and shut the door, then looked me over, still wearing that little grin.

I couldn't help but chuckle.

She laughed too, covering her mouth to snort at her own goofiness. "Come on, Viv and Constance are waiting in the living room for you."

I followed her to the living room where a tray of drinks and snacks sat on the table along with a small stack of magazines and newspapers. I swept the room, nodding at Viv who sat in a pink shirt and white shorts, with a thick afro of curls. When I finally saw Constance, I got that dumb feeling in my chest again.

She was perched on the sofa like a doll; hair pulled back in a neat bun, her vibrant brown skin glowing in the summer sun against her powder blue dress. I tried not to feel nervous when I looked at her, but I couldn't help it. She could look right through me, and I had no idea how to combat that. Thankfully, Constance glanced away before I did.

"Well, well," Viv said, "if it isn't the man of the hour. Literally, you're all over the place, Keem."

"I am?"

"Yes," Keesha exclaimed as she marched over to her seat.

"Come sit down." She waved, and I took a seat in a comfy chair right across from Constance. "Look at this," Keesha said, setting down a magazine.

My eyes almost fell from their sockets when I saw Constance and me on the front cover. Someone had caught the exact moment I'd extended my hand to Constance, trying to get her attention. But somehow, the image made it look more romantic than it was. I'd literally called her three times and I thought she was about to explode into a fit. I only extended my hand as a last attempt to get her attention.

"Wow," I scratched my head, "that's a good angle for us. I guess."

"You two look amazing," Vivian said, smiling hard.

Before I could answer, Constance spoke up. "You see what they're saying about us?"

I raised an eyebrow, unsure I wanted to know.

Constance told me anyway, with an odd look on her face. "They're saying we're in love."

"Which means you two should keep this up." Keesha flipped through the magazine.

"I agree."

My eyes shot to Vivian who was scrolling her phone. No one seemed particularly shocked by the claims in that magazine. They seemed pleased by it. I didn't know how to react at all, so I kept quiet while Viv went on.

"Social media is eating this up," she said. "They love Constance's resilience, and they love you too, Keem. They think," she paused to make big air quotes with her free hand,

"'He's perfect for her. Keem is the perfect gentlemen. We all need a Keem in our life.'"

My sweaty hands were gripping my pants as I tried to figure out how to respond. "I didn't know any of this was happening. I don't have social media," I confessed.

"It's poisonous." Viv grimaced. "You're better off without it."

"Forget the social media," Keesha interrupted, "we need to discuss how these two will keep up this act."

An awkward silence shushed us all as Constance and I both decided this was the perfect time to stare at the floor together. I didn't know what to say, and I didn't know how she'd feel about pretending to be my girl.

I didn't mind since Constance was very business focused, she'd probably only call me for dates, and I wouldn't actually see her outside of those engagements. But what if she *wasn't* okay with it? Why was *I* okay with it?

I barely knew her, though I knew she was a good woman. She'd paid off a debt we'd been slowly chipping away at. She made sure I enjoyed the night out with her, and she even let me keep that suit. But that's all I knew of her. Everything else was tabloid gossip or a total mystery.

"I don't—" Constance and I spoke at the same time, and I stopped to let her speak first.

"I don't think Joaquin has the time for this, and I also don't think it's necessary. It's one magazine, and some social media posts." She shrugged, never making eye contact with me. "What good are those anyway?"

"Connie, you know as well as I do that having support is necessary when you're the small fish in the pond," Vivian countered. "You're building a new business, and people will be interested in it if they know who's running it."

"I don't need people knowing my personal business just to make deals. It'll make me look childish to these companies, like I'm chasing a social media presence and not real business."

"You need to have some sort of presence if you want the public to buy stock again."

"And what if I don't?"

"Guys," Keesha finally interjected. Vivian shook her head as she sat back in her chair. Constance just sighed, allowing Keesha to stare them both down in the silence. "Social media isn't the be all end all, but I can see your point, Viv. Having a little drama will get people interested in the company. It's why you went on this date anyway, to get attention so people would buy your stock, Connie. But," Keesha continued, "I also understand Constance's point too. You don't *need* social media to build a business. It's nice, but Connie is giving this business to the Lord, and she's going to do things differently from everyone else. She's not going to be fake just to get ahead."

"What do *you* think, Keem?" Vivian asked.

I bit my lip, dropping my vision to the floor again. "Whatever Connie wants, I'm cool with."

"You sure?"

I couldn't stop myself from sighing, and at the same time, I lifted my head to see Constance. "I want her to do what she thinks is best. Besides, I'm not in this business, so I don't know how any of this stuff works."

"Do you want to keep seeing Constance?"

Viv was so direct. The question made me a little uncomfortable. I didn't know how to answer. If I said yes, they'd take it the wrong way, and maybe I would too. Connie was a beautiful woman, I wouldn't mind seeing her again, even just as friends. But if I said no, everyone would think I was a selfish brat who just chased after Connie for her money.

"Well, it's not that I don't want to see Connie..." I nodded, trying to put the words together in my head before they reached my mouth. "I do want to see her. I think she's nice. But I don't want to put any pressure on her to see me or allow me to see her. She's starting her own business, and it's been a lot of fun this last week or so, but we're just two strangers who helped each other out. Is there really anything more to us than that?"

"There could be," Keesha said softly. It was the softest she'd ever spoken since I'd met her. "I think you two need each other, honestly. As friends or," she lifted her magazine to me, "as lovers."

My eyes found Connie first, before I realized it was a picture of *both* of us. I was holding her, and she was gazing up at me. I had no idea what I was doing. She looked like she was losing it, like if the wind had blown, she would've been carried away with it. She didn't take my hand and had barely responded when I'd called to her that night.

It was a moment I couldn't forget, and all that evening, I replayed it in my mind, wondering if I'd gone too far. But it'd felt right. Holding her, her hands against my chest, her eyes pleading with me to rescue her. It was fulfilling, and every time I think about that entire night, this moment that's been captured forever is the one I always linger on.

"Would you put that down," Constance was grimacing when she snatched the magazine from a laughing Keesha.

"You two really do look great there. I'm not sure which one is my favorite between the cover photo and this photo." Keesha took the magazine back from Connie.

I didn't have much to say about that. The photos were stunning, and we really did look amazing, but I couldn't force Connie to keep pretending. Besides, it wasn't good to lie, and with the fragile state Connie was in, she'd probably be more closed off than she was during that dinner. The moments the paparazzi had captured were just moments. They caught us at a good time. But if they'd caught us a few days earlier when Connie was crying and I was trying to encourage her, what would've been said then?

Would we still be lovers or just friends?

"Well," I said, after a moment of silence, "I really appreciate you guys inviting me over to see the magazine. I think the pictures turned out really nice." I stood to leave but Constance waved a hand.

"Hold on," she said. "You think the pictures turned out nicely?"

I glanced back down at them. "We looked nice. But I think it was that moment that made those pictures so gripping. Any couple could take pictures like that, but what was happening between us—our connection to each other," I looked up, and Constance's eyes were wide in disbelief, "that's what was captured. And I think it turned out nice."

"Girl, if you don't marry this boy today." Keesha clapped her hands. "I am going to marry him myself! Did you just hear what he said about y'all? Y'all had a *moment*. Y'all had a *connection*!" She stopped to squeal.

Her excitement was cute but also overwhelming. I was starting to get nervous again. I'd clearly said too much.

"I have to say, I'd love to hear my boyfriend talk about our pictures being special like that too." Viv nodded. "But I do agree with Keem. We see couples stand together like that all the time, but what was happening between you two, what was being conveyed here, that's what was captured. Whatever was going on, the secret words between you two, the look in both of your starry gazes makes these pictures worth a thousand words."

Constance was perfectly still, peering down at the photos. When she didn't say anything, I took that as my cue to leave. I gave the other ladies a nod before cramming my hands into my pocket and turning away.

"Hold on," Constance called.

I stopped, turning to face her.

"I think there's grounds for us to be friends, don't you?"

I smiled a little. "I think so."

She nodded, and Keesha and Viv looked satisfied.

10

Constance

Man | Lost | Broken |

"This is Gavin," Vivian introduced her boyfriend to Keesha and me a week after Keem and I decided to become friends. We don't talk at all, I just felt bad for sending the kid home with no answer. That's what I tell myself anyway.

I don't want to dwell on Keem, and I definitely don't want to text him or call him. It would be too confusing. Occasional house visits from him are fine because we need to at least touch base with each other. My friends are always around, so we wouldn't be alone if he visited. But who is to say what would happen on a late-night call or through text messages?

Don't get me wrong… I'm an adult, I can handle being alone with a man. I can handle phone calls and text messages too. I did that with my ex-husband, and we made it to the altar with our purity intact. But this wasn't about *purity*. I wasn't afraid of losing control and giving Joaquin a lap dance. I was afraid of being genuinely attracted to him in the first place.

For my own heart and sanity, keeping our distance was the safest way to go.

"Is this the tech guy who *somehow* knew accounting information?" I asked as I slurped my berry juice.

Gavin chuckled. "Sorry, boss. Viv said it was important."

"Well, nice to know you're loyal to some authority," I said.

"It all worked out in the end." Gavin waved his big, nut-brown hands in the air as if I should just let this all go.

I have let it go, but bringing him back onto our team seemed fishy.

"We're starting over," I said to him. "You can't go mingling in the accounting business if we're bringing you on board. That means staying in your lane and handling tech business only. Unless *I* say otherwise."

"Done." He jerked his head forward, which I recognized as a very enthusiastic nod. "No more mingling and I'll let my brother know you guys are interested."

"Interested in what?" Keesha finally spoke up. She'd been snacking on my cucumbers and feta cheese the entire meeting, offering very little input.

"In my brother's accounting firm." Gavin looked confused for a moment. "Viv said you guys needed an accountant."

I shot Viv a look, but she glanced off.

"Well," I hoped I didn't sound annoyed, "I guess it's fine since we do need an accountant. I wish I'd been informed we'd already had one."

"Is he reputable?" Keesha asked.

Gavin rubbed his palms together. "I mean, we're just a few folks getting together to start a business."

"Ok, so that's a no." Keesha rolled her eyes.

"He's new to the business," Viv said in his defense, "but I think it'd be a good opportunity since we are just starting out."

"Which is why a more seasoned accountant is important here. We need our books done right; we can't start off bad. We've got to hit the ground running in every area if we're going to want investors." I folded my arms, but Viv countered me again.

"Well, if you're going to be a privately traded company this time, then we actually don't need things to be too pristine right now. We can let those who'll understand that we're new buy into us."

"What kind of business plan is that?" Keesha fired. "We're trying to make money, Viv, not just take care of you and your boyfriend and his brother."

"It isn't like that." Viv scowled at Keesha as Gavin raised his hands sheepishly.

"It's alright, ladies," he said. "I'll just tell him we're going in a different direction."

"No, we'll take your brother," I spoke up. "You, Viv, and your brother will be our administration and accounting team. Keesha will cover marketing, and I'll be the one handling deals and other business."

"Really?" Viv smiled as she clutched Gavin's sleeve.

I nodded. "Yes. But everyone's job for now will be to

secure some new business for us and office space. We really don't want to be meeting in homes."

"I agree," Gavin said.

"Well," I extended a hand to Gavin, "welcome to the team."

"Thanks, Mrs. James, I can't wait to get—"

Viv smacked Gavin in the stomach so hard, he coughed on reflex. "It's Ms. *Wells*," she seethed through gritted teeth.

"It's alright." I waved a hand, glancing away from Viv's apologetic look. "I think that's enough for today. We'll officially meet again in two weeks since Keesha's going out of town for funeral business. But if anyone needs me, I'll be here."

A sore smile stretched across Gavin's face as he nodded, taking Viv's hand to lead her out. Lowered brows told me Vivian was aching to apologize, but I refused to look at her as she left. I wasn't angry about Gavin's slip-up; it's just that it was easier not to talk about it at all.

The two left, leaving Keesha and me in silence.

"I'm surprised you didn't cry," she taunted, but I didn't let her words make me angry.

"Me too," I muttered honestly.

"Come on, Connie, when are you going to get over Danny? It's been over six months already."

"He was my husband, Keesha, not my *boyfriend*."

"I know."

I turned on the couch to see her nibbling on a handful of grapes. "Then you should know how hard it is to just stop loving your spouse. Marriage is deeper than a boyfriend."

"I know."

"Why is that your only response?"

"Because you still need to get over him."

"What's with you tonight?" I stood from the couch.

"You still want to be Mrs. James, that's my problem tonight."

"Seriously?"

"Yes." She popped another grape into her mouth and munched it before she stood too. "You're still stuck on Danny, stuck on being his wife. He's gone, Connie. Wake up."

"Don't you think I know that? I'm dealing with this every day!"

"No, you're not," she snapped. "You're throwing yourself a pity party every day about why it's Jada and not you. But who really cares?"

"*I* care, Kee!" I pressed my hand to my own chest, unsure if I was outraged or hysterical. Everything Keesha said was true, but also not true. I knew I needed to get over Danny, but what was wrong with getting over him at my own pace? What was wrong with grieving the love we once had?

Just let me heal in peace...

I took a calming breath and hoped my voice didn't shake as I said, "He left without a word to me. I loved him, Keesh. And one day he just wasn't there anymore. Daniel was my entire life. He was all I knew. Everything I learned about this industry I learned from him. What am I supposed to do now?"

"Grow up," she said coldly. "You can't give him all the

credit. You may have learned from him, but you excelled with *God*. He kept you and took you all the way here. Even when you stopped believing, He was still there."

"I know." I squeezed my eyes shut, whispering, "I know."

"So, when are you going to start being *Ms. Wells*?"

"I don't even know who that is," I mumbled.

"Well maybe it's time you found out."

I opened my eyes to find Keesha setting down a magazine. It was the one from a week ago with Keem and me on the front cover.

"Seriously?" I snatched the magazine from the table and tossed it across the room. "That's all you're interested in, Kee! You don't care about me. You just want drama or something to read about!"

Keesha pouted, her full lips turning downward as she glanced over her shoulder at the magazine in the hall. "I like my gossip as hot as my tea. I'll admit that. But there's more to it than chitchat, Connie. You were smiling in those pictures." Slowly, Keesha moved from the couch and retrieved the magazine. "I just wanted to show you the smile you had. I wanted you to see who Constance Wells really is."

She set the magazine down without a word and flipped it open, pointing to a picture of Keem and me at dinner. "Look at you. You're smiling. This boy brought that out of you. He brought you back to your faith and in one night, he brought a smile out that's been hidden for the last six or seven months."

"It doesn't mean anything," I said as I stared at the picture through blurry tears.

"Yes, it does. But you're too afraid to acknowledge it," Keesha said. "You're afraid because the only person you can't trust right now is *you*."

I closed my eyes as a tear rolled down my cheek. Keesha was right. I couldn't trust Danny, but he's gone now. I couldn't trust Keem at first, but after getting to know him, I've learned he really is a good man. This is about me now. Trusting myself. Trusting that God is with me in my pain and my confusion.

"It's been so hard watching you struggle." Kee sounded like she was going to cry, but I didn't open my eyes. I kept them closed as I listened to her. "You've tried to be strong, and I think in some ways you've gotten there. But, Connie, when you came down the stairs and into the foyer that night, you were glowing like an ember. In those pictures, you are smiling like Danny never existed. That's what I want for you again."

I pressed my hands to my face and sniffled loudly. "But he's just a *boy*, Kee."

"And you're just a girl. No one is saying fall in love with the kid. Just give him a call. Give yourself a chance to let go of Danny."

"Use him," I said angrily, but Keesha shook her head.

"Talk to him. Let him make you laugh, let him tell you more about himself just to give you something else to think about when you're alone."

"I'm scared, Kee." I finally crumbled and sat on the couch, crying heavily into my hands. "I'm scared! I'm scared to let anyone in! I'm scared to befriend anyone. I'm scared to talk to them because—what if I start to feel things again? What if I feel things and he doesn't? What if he fakes like Danny did for the last two years of our marriage? I can't go through this again, Keesha."

"And you won't if you learn to trust yourself. You already trust God, but now you have to learn to trust *yourself*."

"How can I do that if I don't even know who I am without Danny?"

"By finding out." She sat beside me. "Connie, you're the smartest and most beautiful woman I know. You're an entrepreneur. You can start over, and over, and over again if it means getting it right. But you've got to start. You've got to put the key into the ignition and start the car again."

I wiped at my tears, sniffling and trembling in Keesha's embrace. She's been by my side this entire time and she's always had good advice, considering Keesha's only had one boyfriend her entire life. Somehow, she had all the right information on men, and she always knew what to say, even before I met Danny.

"How do I put the key into the ignition? Where do I even find a key?"

"By getting rid of all the old. No one puts new wine into old skins, it'll burst. Do you know why?"

I didn't answer, silently mulling over the Scripture she'd just quoted.

"Because wine ferments. It bubbles, it releases gas. In an old wineskin, the fermentation process will make the entire skin burst because it can't absorb the gases or take the pressure.

But a new wineskin can."

"So, what are you saying?"

"I'm saying that a new fermentation process can't start in you if you're an old skin. Shed that skin. Get rid of it." She did a little motion, pulling at herself as if she was pulling her skin off, and tossed it away. "Let the fermentation process start over again. You've got to smile again if you want to become a nicely aged wine. Yeast needs sugar, which means you need some good times, some *sweet* times, to give that yeast something to convert into alcohol."

"But we don't drink alcohol."

"That doesn't mean it isn't useful. Besides, the point of this whole thing is to get you to start getting rid of the old Constance, and that begins upstairs."

I raised a brow as I sat up from her embrace. "Upstairs?"

"Yes," she sighed, "you need to get rid of his things, girl."

My shoulders sagged. "I know, I just can't—"

"*Couldn't*," she corrected, "but now you can. You can move on, Constance, no one is going to be mad if you do. Not even Danny."

"I know that," I almost snapped.

"Well, I just want you to be prepared for the headlines tomorrow." She patted my shoulder before standing.

"What headlines?" I could feel anxiety digging into my chest as I watched her pack her things, still not answering me. With a shout, I demanded, "What headlines!?"

"Jada's pregnant."

"What?" My ears began to ring. For a second, the room

was silent. I could see Keesha's mouth moving but I couldn't hear the words until she gently shook my shoulder.

I blinked. "What did you say?"

She hesitated but told me anyway. "A friend from an old job sent me an email this morning. She got the inside scoop on Daniel and Jada."

A slip of paper brushed against my hand, and I realized, in a daze, that Keesha had passed me something.

I stared down at the paper, not moving to take it. I *couldn't* take it.

Keesha sighed and read it herself. "Hey, KeeKee, are you still friends with that Constance lady? If so, you better put her on before this drops. Love, Kayla." She paused. "The headline says, **'I'm finally getting my son.'**"

I clutched my belly and tried to catch my breath. "They're having a *son*?"

"I'm so sorry, Connie."

I shook my head, feeling a hot sticky ball form in my throat, clogging up all of my emotions. I didn't care about the child being a *boy*, but I knew Danny did. He'd wanted a son throughout our entire marriage. A girl wouldn't have satisfied him because a girl couldn't be his heir. That's the man I couldn't get over. That's the man who is the cause of the tears that streak my cheeks as I moan in agony. He's a monster, and I'm still not over him.

So, what does that make me?

"I had three miscarriages," I whispered, finally finding my voice. "Three times, he took life from me. Trying to get his boy."

"Connie…" Kee sounded as hurt as I was. "Baby girl—"

"I had *three* miscarriages! And now he's having a son!" I sobbed loudly as I curled over, rolling to the floor. Keesha was at my side in a flash as I wept. "She's been everything I couldn't be," I choked. "But I don't even know who else I *could* have been, and that's why it hurts. It hurts so bad! I can't breathe! I can't *breathe!*" The sobbing made my entire body ache, the tears wouldn't stop flowing.

"What could I have done?" I whined into Keesha's embrace. "Who could I have been for him? I would've been anyone if he'd just asked me!"

"You're stronger than this, Constance," Keesha was saying into my ear as I cried loudly. "You're so much stronger than this. Don't let it break you. Please don't let this break you."

But it was too late.

I am broken.

11

Constance

"A time to weep, and a time to laugh; a time to mourn, and a time to dance; a time to cast away stones, and a time to gather stones together." I paused and reread verse five again. "A time to cast away stones, and a time to gather stones together. What does that mean?"

I'd been meditating on **Ecclesiastes 3:1-8** since I found out that Jada was pregnant with Danny's son two weeks ago. The entire time Keesha was gone, I tried working on myself. Getting rid of Danny's clothes, tossing out everything on his dresser. Our bedroom still looked like he lived there until recently. I'd left things the same in the hopes of his return. But that had to change.

"Who casts stones and gathers them?"

Silently, I moved from the windowsill, and sat at my computer desk. I began to research stones, and what they meant. With a concordance online, I discovered the word 'stones' referred to in this verse was also the *stones* referred to in **I Samuel 17:40**, where David picks up five smooth stones.

Each one of those stones represented something we needed to build our life upon; faith, obedience, prayer, service, and the Holy Spirit. David possessed all five of these attributes as he ran at Goliath, including having the Holy Spirit. Technically speaking, God had always been with David since the Holy Spirit had fallen in the Old Testament, but God's faithfulness was indicative of the Holy Spirit being with *us* in our lifetime.

But the stones, that's what really caught my attention.

The word *stones* in Hebrew had been the same across those verses because they referred to *building*. Which is why we build upon the five principles of David's smooth stones. But even as I researched deeper, I didn't quite understand why someone would cast away stones for building. Scholars said casting stones from a vineyard was probably the interpretation along with rebuilding something, but I didn't think so. Each of these seasons Solomon mentioned came with something positive, and something negative. Removing stones from a vineyard would be positive, but so would gathering stones to rebuild, so I dug a little deeper.

"Huh…" I sat back in my chair and tapped my pencil on my notebook. "The Greek word for 'castaway' means to throw down, or to get rid of. Which would mean throwing down or getting rid of something that was previously built. But the passage never said a time to gather stones *again*, the words wouldn't have been Greek, they'd be in Hebrew and the verse just said to *gather*… which means you're not rebuilding anything at all. You're gathering stones together to build something completely *new*."

Hunching forward, I began to write down my findings. Casting away the stones in the first part of that verse meant getting rid of the things we've built up in our lives. The altars we've set up. But the part about gathering stones means building something, and it all made sense.

Keesha had told me that old wineskins can't hold new wine; you needed *new* wineskins. And it was the same here. There was a time to tear down all the walls you've built yourself to allow God to build things within us. There would be a season of tearing down all your Jerichos, and then there would be a season of building a new altar for God, like the way Noah did when he first stepped onto dry land.

He rededicated the earth to God by building a new altar, and I needed to do the same. I needed to build a new altar with my life for Christ *without* Danny's workmanship.

"And David's smooth stones," I whispered as I wrote, "they were smooth because they were proof that God had protected before and would protect again. A stone is not smoothed naturally, it takes constant wearing and erosion to smooth it, which is like constantly overcoming your trials with God. Smoothing the stone." Turning the page, I finished my notes. "And Jesus is the rock upon which we build ourselves. A rock is made of stone and minerals. Which means Jesus Himself encompasses faith, obedience, prayer, service, and the Holy Spirit."

Setting my pen down, I read over the notes. It was all

starting to make sense, and it felt so freeing. I knew I had to make a decision. I had to let go of Danny, but could I really? Could I really walk away from the man who'd made me who I am? Maybe I'm giving him too much credit like Keesha said. Or maybe I'm not. Daniel may have made me the way I am today, but today, I had to cast away that person.

I'd read somewhere in a book once about a young woman who rose to leadership when her father-in-law died. The only word of advice someone had given her was to kill the girl inside, or rather, *grow up*. That part of the story had always stuck with me, but now it was more than just some character's story, it was my reality. It was time to grow up; time to trust God completely on a new level.

I could trust God in this new way because I've seen Him being a restorer. I've seen Him being a heart regulator, and a peace giver to those in my life. I've tasted God's goodness, and I've seen with my own eyes what He can do. And if He did it for them, He'd do it for me.

All day, I spent my time praying and getting rid of Danny's things. I never wanted freedom before, but now I do. Not just freedom from the pain and shame of my divorce, I wanted to be free from Daniel. I wanted to disassociate with him. I needed this.

I'd been clinging to a false hope that Daniel would return. In my anger, I belittled myself, and everyone else too. But most of all, I couldn't come to terms with my husband leaving me for someone else… typical, but I was prideful.

I was Constance James. I was perfect, or so I believed. But

this divorce showed me just how *imperfect* I was. I needed a conversion, a transformation, a tearing down of all the walls I'd built up in my pride. And now that I had it, I wouldn't let it go... I just couldn't.

Later that day, after some heavy cleaning and packing, I brought down a bag of Danny's old clothes and tossed them into the growing pile at the bottom of my steps. It was after eleven at night now, and I hadn't eaten much. I gave my driver, Bernandad, a call, asking him to meet out front. I was in the mood for steak tacos.

The car ride was long, but Bernie gave me good conversation all the way. He asked about Keesha—he's had the biggest crush on her since I hired him—and I told him she should be back in town. His face was delighted, and he went on to tell me about how wonderful she is. We made a plan together for me to invite Keesha out and he'd drive us around all night. It was cute, though I was positive Kee had never paid Bernie much attention. They'd met on a few occasions, but nothing major.

Bernie took me to my favorite 24-hour taco place. It was an outdoor kind of eatery; a big building surrounded by a parking lot, and you had to walk up and order at the window. There was always Mexican music playing loudly on a speaker, and young couples making out in their cars—school skippers and twenty-somethings trying to steal a passionate moment before life's responsibilities caught up with them. I hadn't been to this place in a while, but as we arrived, I realized nothing had changed. Young people were still making out and Mexican music was still booming.

"Would you like me to grab your favorite, Ms. Wells?" Bernie asked.

"I've got it, Bernie. You want something?"

He shook his head. "No, ma'am, but thank you."

I nodded as I slid out of the car and made my way to the counter. There were a few people in line, giving me a chance to look over the menu. I always ordered steak tacos, but the toppings were so hard to pick from. Did I want a stomachache or a burning butt? Those were always my two options when it came to tacos.

"Constance? Is that you?"

I turned around, and everything I'd spent all day meditating on felt like it had sunk into the ground.

"Daniel," I said quietly.

He skipped through the line and stood beside me. "You look," he snorted, "well."

"What are you doing here?" I asked as I looked back at the menu. It took everything in me not to scream and run away.

"I'm just ordering tacos for me and my hungry fiancée. She's pregnant, so you know how the cravings go," he paused, "or maybe you don't."

I swallowed. "No, I'm not sure."

He nodded thoughtfully. "You've never been good at keeping things together."

My hands balled into fists, but Danny cut me off before I could snap something nasty at him.

"Well, I do have to say ... you did a bang-up job on the company. Selling your stock with all that drama surrounding it, that was a good one."

"Glad you're keeping score," I grinded out.

He grunted as we moved forward in line. "I'm giving you a compliment, Connie. You should take it. It's the only thing you'll ever get from me again."

"I'm not looking for anything from you."

"Come on," he chuckled, "you're obviously looking for something—going out with that valet boy."

I stepped forward, keeping pace with the line, trying to focus on anything but Daniel's antagonizing words. I was hoping that either the line would move quicker, or Bernie would come rescue me, but so far neither of those scenarios were playing out.

God, I don't think I can do this.

Remember the smooth stones.

I clutched my fist, trying to follow His Voice and remember what each one stood for, but I couldn't. I couldn't tune Danny out. He was beside me and my heart was racing yet breaking at the same time. This wasn't the Daniel I remembered. The man I married wasn't evil or callous like this.

"You know something?" Danny snickered. "I'm the happiest I've been in all five years of our marriage. Finding out Jada was pregnant was better than our wedding day."

He's just trying to get under my skin. I took a breath to still myself.

"And, man, the sex we have," he leaned closer to whisper,

"it's been—"

"Glad to know you haven't moved on," I finally looked up at him, staring right into his glaring eyes.

That's when I saw it. Jealousy.

All this time, I thought I hadn't been good enough for Daniel, little did I know, it was the other way around. How had I been so stupid? Daniel had taught me everything, but in those five short years of our marriage I'd managed to learn enough to stand by his side in our business. As his equal.

I'd never given him a son, but I had given him loyalty. I had given him love. I had suffered multiple miscarriages for him—a sacrifice he could never understand. And when that didn't break me, when it proved to him that I was not the weak-minded little girl he fooled during our courtship, he ended things without a word.

I smirked at him, mentally reaching out and clutching a stone in my palm. Faith. Faith in God to move my mountains—or to tear down my enemies.

"What did you just say?" Daniel asked dumbly.

My smirk stretched wider. "All this bragging, going out of your way to compare me to some other woman I don't even know—you've just showed your true colors. You aren't over me. In fact, you're obsessed with me, Daniel. Obsessed with proving that you're better than me."

"I have moved on," he insisted weakly. "And I'm actually happy. Don't try to switch this around to guilt trip me back to you."

"You wouldn't need to make that trip if you weren't wrong

to begin with." I sighed as I looked at him. At this man I had loved. I was stronger now, but I couldn't pretend his words hadn't hurt me. The revelation of his true intentions took some of the sting away, but my heart still stung. I fought with everything in me not to cry, and crumble right there. Not to think about the precious baby boy he's going to have soon, and how I still can't nurture a child of my own.

I shook the thoughts away and lifted my chin. "Daniel, you will never be happy because you're always competing. It wasn't enough to leave me without explanation. You wanted to *hurt* me, and you did. So, what more do you want from me? I'd given you everything before, but I will not do it again." I swept my hair over my shoulder and stepped forward to the counter to order. I didn't care what I ordered and was struggling to even keep a straight face. My appetite was gone, and anxiety and brokenness had replaced it, but I wouldn't let him know it.

I grabbed my order and turned to leave, slamming right into Daniel.

"You want to know why I left?" he snapped. "Because you're nothing, Constance. You've always thought you were perfect for me, and that I was perfect because of you. I was tired of being second to you in everything and in—"

"You're wrong," my voice cracked, "you're so wrong." I pushed by him and headed for my car. When I got in, I slammed the door shut and Bernie called, "Ms. Wells? Are you alright?"

"Just take me home please." I reached up and pulled the

partition shut.

I wouldn't look out the window as we pulled off, I was afraid I'd see Daniel, and he'd see the tears. I couldn't hold them in any longer. I thought I was stronger, I thought I'd gotten better, I thought I was free, but it had only been a day, and I hadn't done much of anything.

In my mind, I grabbed another stone. *Holy Spirit... help me.*

Shakily, I gripped my phone, scrolling through for Keesha's number. I needed to talk to her, I needed her to say something. I hit the name and clutched the phone to my ear. My sobs were quiet as I held them in when I heard the phone pick up.

"Keesha," my voice trembled.

"Connie? What's wrong?"

I blinked. This voice, it isn't Keesha's...

I snatched the phone from my ear and stared at the screen. *Keem.*

I rolled my eyes, suddenly aggravated. Viv had put his number in my phone under *Keem* a few weeks back, and I must've hit it through the tears, trying to call Keesha.

"Hello?" Keem called.

"Yeah," I placed the phone back to my ear.

"You alright?" His voice was low and groggy like he'd been sleeping.

"Yeah," I swallowed, "I'm alright."

He cleared his throat. "It doesn't sound like it. What's going on?"

"Nothing," I tried to sound normal, but the jitters and

nerves had left my voice shaky.

"Well, you called in the middle of the night, it must be something."

"It's not the middle of the night."

"Sorry," he chuckled, it was a deep chuckle that sounded warm and welcoming, "I worked a double from last night through the morning. Got an hour off and went back in and worked overtime until about an hour ago."

"You're working a lot," I said, trying to steer the conversation away from me.

"Yeah, my dad's putting me out in about two weeks, so I've been working overtime every shift."

"What? Why is he putting you out?"

"I'll tell you if you tell me why you called me crying."

My shoulders sank, and I could feel myself smiling a little. "You're good, kid," I whispered.

"I haven't heard from you in weeks, Connie. And the first time I do, you're crying." I could hear him adjusting in bed. "So, what's going on?"

"I … um…" My hand began to tremble as I clutched the phone, but I forced myself to go on. "I saw Daniel tonight. I went for tacos, and he was there. He said a lot of things that I'm struggling with."

"Where are you now?"

"Just going home."

"I'll meet you there."

I shook my head, the sadness ebbing. "No, you just got into bed."

"I'm not working tomorrow." His voice sounded a little more awake. "I can sleep then."

"No, Keem, I'm fine. I just—"

"I want to see you," he said plainly, stopping my heart.

This was exactly the reason I had a no phone call/text rule in place between us. And now, in one swift move, he's breaking my other rule—no house visits without someone else there.

I gulped, not really knowing what to say. The silence between us was filled with Keem's movement; I could hear him grabbing things, walking around, doors and floors creaking. I wanted to turn him away, but he was already up, and I knew he wasn't going to take no for an answer. I could've hung up or made up an excuse to hang up and call Keesha instead. But I didn't want to do that. When I heard Joaquin's voice, I just couldn't put the phone down.

"I'm outside now," he said, calling me back to our conversation after the long silence. "You still there?"

"Yes," I said quietly.

"Good. How are you feeling?"

"Tired."

"Me too." He laughed.

"Joaquin—"

"Connie, I'm already on my way."

"I know."

The silence lingered a while longer, but I listened to his journey. He was panting a little, like he was jogging, moving quickly to come see me. The thought made me smile because I could hear Keesha screaming for joy in the back of my mind.

"How close are you?"

"I'm three minutes away."

"I can't believe you walked all the way here." Though he's done it before, we only met around the same time because the taco place was further away than his home.

"I can't believe you stayed on the phone with me. I'm surprised."

"Well, I didn't want you getting lost, or something," I said.

He laughed again, and I chewed my lip as I leaned my head against the car window. Bernandad was still taking me home from the taco place, that bit of drama seemed like it'd happened hours ago. We pulled around the fountain, and I saw Joaquin standing there waiting, white breath escaping him as he held the phone to his ear.

I hung up as Bernie parked and opened my door for me. For just a moment, I hesitated to step out, staring at the blacktop until Keem's sneakers came into view.

"Connie," he said, extending a hand, "come on."

It reminded me of the moment he'd held out his hand on the steps of The Palace restaurant. Back then, he'd done the same thing. Came to my rescue and called my name to get me to focus again. I had hesitated last time, unsure if I could trust this man not just with my hand but with my heart too. This time, as he reached for me, I took his hand without a second thought. Though my stomach knotted with butterflies.

Keem helped me out of the car and didn't let go as we walked inside. Closing the door, we stood there in the foyer in the dark. The light from outdoors snaked inside through the curtains, but we didn't move, we just stood there. I couldn't get myself to move. I couldn't get myself to do anything but stand beside him ... until he moved.

"Constance," he pulled me towards him, and I stumbled into his embrace.

The moment I fell into his chest, I began to weep. He held me, letting me cry over my ex-husband in his arms. His kindness made me angry, and I shoved away from him.

"What's wrong?" he asked, the moonlight glowing across half his face.

"You're just letting me cry about another man right here."

"I was just—"

"Stop being nice to me! Say something mean! Do something! Do anything!"

He stepped forward and silenced me. He was taller than me, much taller, and in the moonlight, he looked like a man you could only dream of. He leaned closer, examining me slowly, before brushing his lips against my neck.

"Is this what you want?" his voice was a whisper in the silence.

"I don't know."

"Tell me what you want, and I'll do it."

"I don't know what I want," I confessed.

"Ok." He leaned down and swept me off my feet, bridal style.

I clung to him as his eyes danced over me again before carrying me to my big comfy chair in the living room. When he sat, I was in his lap, still clinging to him, and he was cradling me.

"I never told you why my father was putting me out."

Silently, I leaned my head against his chest as he held me there. I hadn't felt like this in a long time.

"We got into an argument," he told me. "And we ended up tussling a little. Then he gave me a month to get out."

"That's why you've been working so hard?"

"Mmhmm." His response came from his chest, and I could feel his words humming through him.

"Is this ... okay?" I asked.

He adjusted to lean back and look down at me. "When you get tired of holding on, I'll still be holding you. You can let go whenever you want."

I clutched him a little tighter. "I ... I don't want to let go."

He took a deep breath, making my own body rise and fall with his chest. "Good."

12

Constance

I sniffled as I floated into consciousness. When I opened my eyes, I had to squint back the sunlight gazing in. Everything felt good, the warm blanket, the morning sun, the body heat...

The body heat?

I jerked up, realizing I hadn't fallen asleep on the couch last night alone. Keem was lying underneath me, his arms lazily folded around my waist, and I was on his chest. I pressed a hand to my chest and sighed within, we still had our clothes on. Last thing I remembered was Keem telling me about his father, and then there are other memories of me crying, but it's all a blur right now.

Carefully, I tried to wiggle free without disturbing him, but his lashes fluttered open, and he sleepily said, "Constance?"

"Yeah?" I whispered back.

"Are you leaving?"

"I have to go to the bathroom."

He inhaled deeply, as if falling asleep again, but his heavy lids blinked slowly as he adjusted beneath me to let me go. Pushing the covers back, I climbed off him, and my bare foot touched the fluffy carpet.

"Connie," he called, catching my hand before I could get away. I glanced back at him, he was still sleepy, but he looked at me with concern. "You'll come back, right?"

I wondered if he was dreaming, but I gave him a small smile and nodded.

"Ok..." He let me go and I walked briskly to the stairs, grabbing my purse from the floor on the way.

I couldn't get up the stairs fast enough. I was panting by the time I made it to my bathroom and shut the door behind me with my foot. This time, I made sure I dialed Keesha's number since I knew it by heart. The phone rang, and rang, and rang.

"Come on, Kee," I whispered, jamming a nail into my mouth to anxiously bite it.

"Hello?"

"Keesha!" I screamed in a husky whisper.

"Constance? What's wrong?" Her voice wasn't drowsy, she sounded alert.

"Keem is at my house," I said.

"What happened to him?" I could tell she was still thinking there was a serious problem, and while it was ... it also really wasn't.

"Nothing—he," I paused, staring at the marble floors of my bathroom.

"He what?" she demanded.

"He stayed the night."

The sheets rustled on the other end, and then she screeched, "What!?"

"I *know*," I whined. My bare feet slapped the cool tile of my bathroom floor as I walked to the long wide counter. It was marble too, when I first had the house built, I was obsessed with the stone.

"You guys had sex?" Kee asked, and I couldn't tell if she was excited or disappointed.

"No," I said quickly, "we just ... we slept together."

"You slept with him but didn't body him down?" Keesha paused. "Girl, what?"

"That's not the Christian way."

"Girl, wasn't nothing biblical about last night already, don't go pointing the finger at my conclusions."

I groaned. "Kee, I'm serious. I'm conflicted because I know it was wrong, but beneath the confliction, I feel a little happy."

"I know you do, that boy is fine."

"Keesha!"

"Ok, ok," she laughed, "enough jokes. Seriously, how did this even happen?"

"Well, funny thing, I was trying to call you last night. But Viv put Joaquin in my phone as *Keem*, and I accidentally called him and not you."

"The fact that you didn't hang up from him immediately and just call me says a lot already."

"It wasn't like that. I needed to talk."

She fell quiet. "What happened, Connie?"

"I'd been doing everything you said; getting rid of Danny's things these whole two weeks. Meditating on scriptures and trying to refocus on God. But, as soon as I saw him, all of it went out the window. I tried to hold onto my scriptures, but he was so ... mean."

"You saw Danny?"

I nodded, though she couldn't see it, and told her how I'd bumped into him at the taco stand.

"What'd he say?" Kee asked.

"He told me that he left me because I was always trying to outdo him or something like that."

"What a liar," Keesha snapped angrily.

"I know. It made no sense. And then he went on about how Jada can have a son and I couldn't. It was just a lot to handle."

"Wow," she scoffed, "you better thank God you called Keem and not me, because I would've gone to Danny's house and got things straight."

I chuckled. "It was so hard to keep a straight face."

"But you didn't cry in front of him, right?"

"No, I cried in the car, which is why I called Keem and not you because I couldn't see with all the tears."

"Did you have a driver?"

I gulped. "Yeah, but I don't think—"

"No, I'm coming over to fire him personally. He should have been there to defend you, or at least chase Daniel away."

Though he'd be satisfied with seeing Kee, I didn't want to

fire Bernie. "Kee, it's fine."

"You're too nice."

"Anyways," I looked into the mirror at myself. My bun was still somewhat neat, but my face looked refreshed, like I hadn't slept this well in years. "Keem came over so I wouldn't be alone."

"He came to comfort you," she said, twisting the details a little, "and stayed all night?"

"Well, technically he came at night."

"Hold on, Keem came to your house at *night?*"

I sighed. "It was close to midnight when I called him."

"And he came over anyway?"

"Yes, and it gets worse."

"No, baby girl, it doesn't."

"He told me he wanted to see me, *and* he got out of bed to come see me after working a double shift."

"No wonder he stayed the night. He got up out of the bed to get some—"

"Keesha!"

"I was going to say *fresh air*," she cackled.

"Kee, it was so crazy. He literally jogged to my house."

"How do you know?"

"We... stayed on the phone until he got here."

"Oh no, girl, you just got a boyfriend. I'm coming over."

"Kee, wait a second," I whimpered as I dropped my head into my hand, "the whole night was overwhelming."

"The *whole* night? Well, what happened when he got there?"

"We went inside." I omitted the fact that he walked me in holding my hand. "And when the door closed, I broke down in tears again. And he held me."

The memories vividly flashed in my mind, making me uncomfortable.

"But then I got angry. I was angry at myself for crying, but I took it out on him. Telling him he was too nice and that he should be mean to me, or he should do something besides just stand there and let a woman cry about another man in his arms."

"What did he say to that?"

"He didn't really say anything. He came over to me, and…" I couldn't say it, but I slapped a hand to my neck to stop the tingling I remembered from his lips.

"And what?" Kee insisted. "Don't leave me hanging."

"He whispered right against my neck, Kee, like he was going to kiss it, but he didn't know if it was okay or not."

"Girl, what?"

"And then he asked me if that was what I wanted. For him to be all over me. But I just don't understand. It's like he's a totally different person when he gets serious. Just like on that date. He grabbed me and pulled me into him without hesitation."

"What did you say? Please tell me you told him yes!"

"I told him I didn't know. But then he swept me off my feet like I was his *bride* and carried me to the couch."

"And that's where y'all made love?"

"We didn't do that!" I almost yelled.

"You know you wanted to."

"I don't know what I want anymore."

"Well, it's clearly not Danny."

"Kee, I can't even see the guy without crying."

"Maybe if Keem was there, you might be able to."

I sighed, but I didn't respond as I sat on the counter. I thought Keesha was right. Maybe if Keem was there, I wouldn't feel so weak. But I didn't want to depend on another man for my strength. I wanted God to be my strength.

"So, what's the real problem, Connie?"

"I'm nervous. What if I like him?"

"Then date him," she said nonchalantly.

"Keesha, we're almost seven years apart."

"And?"

"And he's a valet boy."

"Ouch, that's shallow, sis."

I rolled my eyes. "Come on, we're years apart and worlds apart."

"And that is what's so exciting about all of this. You guys are totally different."

"When that wears off, then what? When he's gotten over being with a loaded older woman, then what, Kee?"

"Then the *real* fun begins," her voice was cunning, like she'd been waiting to make this point. I could practically see her smiling. "Everyone always cries and whines about the fantasy stage in a marriage. About that being the *best time*, but they're wrong. That's the *hardest* time of the relationship. Getting to know someone's likes and dislikes, deciding to change for them or not. Going out of your way until you get tired and who you really are emerges." She snickered. "When you're through with all of that, then you guys really fall in love. You guys laugh like never before, you talk without even muttering a word in a crowd of people. Your late-night conversations mean more because they replaced the hot sex. Speaking of which, sex gets better with age. You'll know Keem's body better after two years verses one late night hookup."

"Goodness," I whispered.

"Come on," she snorted, "a hookup is the worst idea ever. You have no idea what the person likes, and there's no *love* in it. Sex is intimacy because there's an overarching goal; make *each other* feel good and produce a child. But that doesn't happen with a stranger during a hookup. One-night stands are about the individuals, not about the intimacy. Even sex with a boyfriend or girlfriend is different because it takes time to learn what makes him, *ya know*, and what makes you, *ya know*."

"I got it, Keesha."

"Good." She laughed. "So now that you've had my sex education class, what are you going to do?"

"What should I do? I'm nervous that maybe Keem's just here for himself."

"Connie, I know you're a divorcee, but if you treat every man like he's your ex fighting for another chance, you'll never be happy."

"I'm scared, Kee," I whispered into the phone. I could hear her moving around.

"Listen, I'm on my way over there. I'll be there in thirty minutes. For now, just take a bath, relax, and then when I get there, we'll ask him what his intentions are. Does that sound good?"

"Yeah, that sounds good."

"Alright, I'll be there soon. I love you, Constance."

"Love you too, Kee."

When I hung up the phone, I stood from the counter and looked in the mirror a while longer. I was weak, but I wanted to be strong. I was scared, but I wanted to be bold.

Reaching out, I pressed a hand to the glass. "I have to do it myself. I can't depend on Keesha, or anyone else but God."

I swallowed and backed away from the mirror to shower. I knew Keesha meant well, but this was a conversation I needed to have with Joaquin myself. For my own sanity, I needed to know for certain that he was here for money, and he didn't want anything serious so that my heart could move on. I'd convinced myself otherwise because he was so nice, but what if he was just like Danny? What if Keem's just been pretending? Have I been fooled by a kid?

After my shower, I followed my winding staircase down and found my way to the living room where Keem was still sleeping. I'd changed out of my clothes, freshened up, and put on a robe and a lace nightie. Then I approached Keem. He looked comfortable, his angled jaw was relaxed, and he was sleeping soundly.

"Keem," I whispered as I touched his shoulder.

He grunted.

"Keem," I whispered again, swiping a hanging curl behind my ear.

He took a deep breath before his eyes opened. "Connie," he smiled, "you came back."

"I did." I lifted the blanket so I could snuggle with him again. With a deep breath, I set one leg on either side of his hips and settled onto his lap. The gentleness that was always in his eyes resurfaced as the sleepiness wore off.

"Is this what you want, Keem?" I asked. "Is this why you're here?"

He squinted, and then he sat up a little, placing a hand on my cheek. "This isn't you, Connie."

"Stop it." I pushed his hand away and shoved him back into the couch. "Tell me that you're here for sex. Tell me that you're only nice because you want something from me."

"No." He shook his head, but when I reached for his pants, he grabbed my hands and snapped, *"Constance!"*

"Is this what you want!?" I shouted. "You're not here for me!"

I yanked my hands free and tore at my robe, trying to get it off as tears burned my eyes.

"Constance, stop it," he said softly, but I didn't listen. "Constance!"

"Why?" I shouted. My robe slipped down my arm, exposing some of my lace gown. I should've been crying because it was sheer, and I knew he could see my body through it, but I was crying because I was scared. "Why won't you be who you really are?" I hiccupped.

"Constance," he lifted my chin, "this is who I really am. I'm not going to change. I'm not going to turn my back on you. I know you're scared, but all I have is my word. If that's not enough, then tell me what I need to do to prove to you that I care about you. How can I make you believe me?"

I blubbered and fell into his chest, sobbing like a child. It was okay. It was all okay. There was a foreign feeling of relief gently brushing over me. I didn't know if it was okay to be happy again. I didn't know if it was okay to get over Danny, but right now, in Keem's embrace, it felt alright.

He adjusted, holding me against him as we lay there. "Do you remember when we moved to the couch last night?"

"We… moved?" My voice was shot after the sobbing.

"Yeah, we fell asleep in one of those big chairs, but then I woke up, and you were on the couch crying. I couldn't get you to stop, so I stayed there with you."

"I remember now. I couldn't sleep, I just kept crying, and then you sat with me for a while, until you hugged me, and we fell asleep like that."

"Yeah." His voice was a whisper now. "I stayed because I care, Constance. I don't have any other reason or motive for being here."

13

Joaquín

Happy Birthday

A horn blared, jerking Connie and me from our slumber. We'd fallen asleep on the sofa again after that crazy early morning event. Constance was still in her nightie, which honestly looked great on her, but the sight of it reminded me of her tears and her insecurities. I wouldn't dare ogle her in this state—I had too much respect for her to do that. But I did pull her closer for just a moment, and then that moment was ruined by another blaring car horn.

Connie jerked upright, blinking wildly, like she had no idea where she was or what was going on. "What was that sound?" she whispered.

"Sounded like a car—"

"Oh no…" She slid off of me and ran out of the living room.

For a moment, I didn't move. I had no idea what to do. Then I heard Connie's voice; she was speaking quickly, and she sounded frustrated. The voice responding to her sounded just as angry—and it was moving toward the living room.

I sat up and tried to smooth the wrinkles in my shirt, but nothing could wipe away the sleepy look on my face. By the time I rubbed the crust out of my eyes, Constance and her angry guest were in the room with me.

"What is going on here?" Keesha snapped, gesturing to me.

Connie set her hands on her hips. "Why on earth were you laying on your horn, Keesha? You could've woken the neighbors."

"Did I interrupt something?" She raised an eyebrow, making me glance away in shame.

Connie didn't feel embarrassed at all. She lifted her chin. "You didn't interrupt a thing."

I wasn't sure if I should be offended or not.

"You two were sound asleep on the couch," Keesha pointed out.

"Yes." Connie shrugged. "What is your point?"

"My point is that I waited over an hour for someone to open the door because I forgot my key. Then Bernie showed up—thank God, he let me inside—and I walk in to find you two snuggled up!"

"What time is it?" I asked.

"Time for you to go home, kid," Keesha said gruffly.

"Hold on," Connie folded her arms over her full breasts, pulling her robe closed at the same time. "It was an accident, Kee. Why send him home?"

Keesha rolled her eyes and walked away. "Unbelievable."

"*Kee*," Connie whined, then she turned to me. "She'll get over it."

I nodded as I stepped into my shoes. "I think I overstayed anyway."

"No, you were fine."

"You sure? Keesha seems really upset."

She laughed. "I told you; she'll get over it."

"Alright." I took a chance and leaned over to kiss her cheek. To my surprise, she didn't pull away from me, instead, Connie glowed like a firefly in the deepest part of the night as I pulled away.

She avoided looking at me as she asked, "Do you want to stay for breakfast? You can freshen up in the bathroom."

I hesitated. "Do you want me to stay for breakfast?"

She hesitated *longer*. "Y-Yes."

"Then I'll stay."

"There's a guest bathroom down the hall, it's got supplies in there. I'll meet you in the dining room afterward."

"Sounds good."

After freshening up, I found Constance exactly where she said she'd be; in the dining room with Keesha and a full buffet of eggs, bacon, pancakes, hashbrowns, buttermilk biscuits—you name it.

"Wow…" I sat on one of the barstools at the island in the middle of the kitchen. "Everything looks amazing."

Connie smiled shyly, but Keesha didn't speak.

I gulped. "Um, Kee, are you still—"

"Yes," Keesha replied tersely, then she scooped eggs onto her plate and made a show of turning her back to me so she could get bacon from the sizzling skillet on the stove.

I passed Connie a grin, and for the first time, we shared a silent exchange. Connie's eyes filled with laughter as I grinned, trying not to laugh at Keesha. This felt so new yet familiar at the same time. Constance and I hadn't known each other for long or very well, but she had suddenly become very important to me.

Last night, when I heard her crying on the phone, I couldn't get myself to calm down. A knot formed in my stomach that forced my legs to run and forced my mind to race without a plan. The only thing I knew to do was reach her, but words weren't enough. Or maybe they *were*, but they weren't enough for *me*.

The knot in my stomach didn't ease until she was in my arms. Everything inside me felt alright when I held her. The relief was like the first breath you take when you emerge from beneath the stormy waves. Holding her was my breath of fresh air, but I don't know when that changed for me. I don't know when she stopped being another rich lady and became the only person who could make me get out of bed through the middle of the night and race to be by her side.

This attraction I felt to her, it was beyond a *crush*, beyond simply *liking* her. It was a connection. When we fell asleep on the couch together, it felt like she was tethered to me, and without her, I'd float away with the wind, completely forgotten.

"What are you two smiling about?" Keesha's voice gripped my attention. I hadn't even realized I was still smiling at Connie.

"We're smiling at you." Connie recovered first, glancing away to smile at her best friend.

Keesha waved a hand. "Love birds in a love nest that I got locked out of."

"We're not love birds." Constance rolled her eyes, but she didn't look at me afterward. Her gaze dropped to her plate, and mine did too.

"Oh, now y'all not smiling anymore," Keesha said.

I glanced up and caught her passing each of us a look with folded arms.

"I'm sorry," I muttered. "I shouldn't have asked her to come back to bed when she wanted to leave initially."

Keesha looked me over, and then cracked a smile. "Alright fine, I'll forgive you just this once, Keem, but next time I'm not going to forgive you so easily."

"I promise to be better." I nodded.

She laughed and winked. "I see you plan to be around more often then."

"Kee, will you let him eat his breakfast?" Connie interrupted, then she turned to me and quickly changed the subject before Keesha could even respond. "What are your plans today?"

I shrugged. "Nothing really. I don't really celebrate my birthday anymore since my mom passed. I would've worked, but I'm exhausted and—"

"Wait a second." Constance raised one of her eyebrows, and I immediately felt like I'd done something wrong. "Today is your birthday?"

"Yeah—why?"

"Because it's your *birthday*!" Keesha frowned. "What do you mean, 'why'?"

I was so used to not celebrating it, I almost couldn't figure out why they'd reacted this way. Dad had stopped caring years ago, but that didn't bother me because I'd stopped too. Mom had been the only birthday stickler in the house, but with her gone, Dad and I just never talked about celebrating.

"Sorry. I only took the day off because I was exhausted," I said.

"You don't celebrate your own birthday?" Keesha asked.

I looked away, swirling a piece of sausage in the syrup on my plate. "Used to, but I don't now."

"Why not?" Connie asked.

"I just don't anymore. Birthday celebrations were something special for Mom, so…" I stopped swirling my piece of sausage and stared at the empty plate. Thinking of Mom was hard, but it was especially hard on my birthday.

The last birthday my mother and I celebrated was when I turned eighteen. She was really sick, but she'd somehow found the strength to surprise me at home. I'll never forget that day; I cried so hard.

My mother hadn't been home in months, and when I came downstairs the morning of my birthday, she was sitting on the couch in the living room with a gift box in her hand. There was a nurse off to the side, and a breathing machine hooked up to my mother, but she was home, and that was the last day she ever spent there.

That memory should make me happy. The fact that my birthday was her last day at home should put a smile on my face, but the word *last* put a damper on things. My last birthday with her, the last day she spent at home, the last time she walked around for more than ten minutes at a time. It was the last time I saw my father really happy, smiling like Mom being home meant that everything was going to be alright.

It wasn't, no matter how hard we tried to fool ourselves that day. The smiles, the cheers, the nurse who chimed in every now and then, my eighteenth birthday was one for the books, and I don't think I'll ever celebrate another birthday again. Just so that this memory wouldn't be forgotten. So that Mom wouldn't be forgotten.

"Keem…" Keesha reached for my hand, but I set my fork down and stood.

"Thanks for everything, Constance, but I think I'd better go."

Connie chewed her lip, a sad look in her eyes. I'd spent the entire night comforting her, but I had no idea how to comfort myself. I'm usually fine, but my birthdays have always been a soft spot for me. I prefer to do them alone. Honestly, I prefer to work all day to avoid the tears and heartache. Today, I had no work, so instead I would indulge in sleeping.

Moving from the table, I gave both ladies a nod and headed for the door.

"Keem," Constance's small feet padded across the floor to me. "You sure you'll be okay alone?"

She looked up at me, and this time the sadness in her eyes wasn't for herself, it was for me. She looked the way my mother always had, forgetting her own pain, and only worrying for mine. I hated that look, but not because I was angry; I hated it because it made me feel useless.

"Don't do that." I stepped back from Connie. "Don't care about me like that."

Constance looked confused, but I promise I felt more confused than she did.

"You look just like her." I shook my head. "Don't worry about me. Please…" My pleas were clutched in my throat, and I was barely able to squeak them out. I didn't get emotional about my mother very often, but it was agonizing when I let the old pain pry its way back into my mind and my heart.

"Joaquin…" Connie reached for me but stopped short. After a second, she retracted her hand into her chest, and then she looked away.

Fear—or *something*—eddied against the main current of her judgement. She didn't want to rub me the wrong way, but she wasn't sure what else to do. Constance hadn't done anything wrong. Her efforts to comfort me weren't vain, I just hated the way it made me feel. I hated how much it made me miss my mother. I hated that concern was no longer innocent for me, it was just a switching mechanism. Concern made me shield everyone off because it scared me.

I was afraid that I couldn't do it… again.

My mother's greatest fear was that I'd never really be able to move forward after her death. She was afraid she'd miss me growing up, and she wouldn't be there for me when things got hard. Mom was afraid that exactly what happened between my father and me would be our new lifestyle.

Distance beyond traveling.

And she was afraid that even if I fell in love, I'd never love the way I was supposed to. I'd give but wouldn't accept. Run myself ragged in the hopes of proving that I loved someone. And all those things were happening. I couldn't keep her fears from reality, I couldn't make myself worth her concern. And I was so afraid that I'd never be worth the concern of anyone else, so I fought against it. I tried to be distant, but then Constance came along and the distance I couldn't travel for my father, for my mother, I realized I could for her… and that scared me too.

Connie backed away like she'd just broken me. I *was* broken, but it wasn't her fault. I'd been broken and trying to heal for a while; some days the healing seemed like it stopped.

"I didn't mean to—"

"It's me, not you, Connie." I nodded and tried to smile, though I knew she saw right through it.

"Okay," she whispered.

I closed the gap between us and kissed her cheek. "Thank you for everything."

14

Constance

"And then he just left," Keesha explained, hopping up to sit on my kitchen counter.

Vivian glanced between Keesha and me. She came to the house with some minor business information to share, but Keesha could hardly wait to tell her about Keem's outburst on his birthday last week.

"So he stayed all night," Viv recalled, "and then his birthday rolled around and he was ready to go? Literally teary eyed—and you didn't go after him?"

Keesha shook her head disappointedly. "That's what I said! He spent all night comforting her, but she didn't comfort him."

"I thought he needed space! Did you see the way he looked at me?" I paused, remembering the way his brows were caught together, a frown on his face. He usually looked youthful and jolly, but just for a second, Keem looked like a man, a broken one doing his best to mend the pieces together. "He's helped me so much, but what have I done for him? He's hurting so much on the inside, trying to be strong, but he isn't." I licked my lips. "What do I do?"

"Aww, Connie…" Viv reached across the table and grabbed my hand. "We'll figure something out."

"Why don't you just call him? You said he wanted to talk to you when you called him by mistake, right?" Kee smiled encouragingly. "Why not start there?"

"You think a call is good enough?"

"You like Joaquin, don't you?"

"No." I let go of Viv's hand and sat up straight. "I don't like him, I-I just want to help him. Return the favor."

"There she is," Keesha laughed, "I thought Constance Wells was finally letting her patchy walls down."

"What?" I crossed my arms. "What do you mean my *patchy walls*? I don't have any walls."

Viv pulled her mug of tea to her lips, speaking over the rim, instead of taking a sip. "There's definitely something keeping you from being with Keem."

"Not you too, Vivian," I whined. "Just because I don't believe he has real feelings for me doesn't mean I don't care about him. I don't have walls up, I'm just not diving headfirst into this."

"I'm just saying," Keesha walked to the table and grabbed a donut from the center plate, "he's a good guy—"

"A good *kid*," I corrected. "Joaquin is a kid."

"Could've fooled me, the way he's handled you." Viv winked, giving me a smirk that made my hand itch to slap it off her face. But I only grunted and pierced Keesha with my stare. It was her fault Viv could make claims like this because she wouldn't stop going on about Keem staying the night and wiping my tears away like that meant something other than what'd actually happened.

Keesha paid my glare no attention. "You know what I think? I think Connie is too afraid to admit to us that she likes Keem."

I rolled my eyes. "Maybe I actually *don't* like Keem." I jolted from the table as Viv and Keesha called for me not to leave. The two of them together were always wearing my nerves down about this man. I'm not even completely over Daniel yet, there was no way I was into Keem. What happened last week was a fluke because of the high emotions. I let my head get too big, but I've been meditating on scriptures again and I'm better now. I won't let myself get smudged over the way I let Daniel's kindness rock me senseless. I couldn't do it again.

I stood out back, leaving Keesha and Vivian to laugh and talk to each other. They were still talking about Keem and me, but I didn't care. I needed a break. I needed fresh air.

Joaquin had become the only topic anyone seemed interested in discussing lately. I couldn't blame them—admittedly, he's all I could think about too. But not because I liked him, it was because he'd been there for me despite not even knowing me that well. He's been good to me, and I wanted to repay him. I just had no idea how.

Stepping off the back ledge, I walked through the grass to

the small house sitting in the fields. There was a glass-enclosed walkway that's heated in the winter and cooled in the summer connecting my place to the housekeepers' home. Two years ago, Danny had a house erected for them. He said it was a good investment since we'd had trouble getting them to be here during certain hours and gone by the time we arrived. It was much easier to hire our own dedicated team of housekeepers and put them on payroll instead of outsourcing through a company. I didn't oppose, it didn't matter to me. I just wanted the house cleaned.

I'd never visited the little cottage, even though I'd let Danny design it himself. It'd been his idea, so I let him handle the project. But neither of us ever had a reason to go in there, so I never gave it much thought. But today, I just wanted to get away from Kee and Viv, and hiking through the grass instead of taking the heated walkway gave me the fresh air I was looking for.

When I got to the door, I pushed it open and let myself inside. I was shocked to find a woman standing there in sweats and a t-shirt. "Ms. Wells, did you call for us?" she asked kindly.

"No." I waved. "I just wanted to hide from my friends. They're so overbearing."

Wide blue eyes blinked as she looked me over. I guess this was the first time she'd ever seen me in person. I had no idea who she was, she could be a killer for all I knew since I'd never met the housekeeping team officially. I only met the woman who'd been hired as the head of the household, making arrangements with Danny or me for the housekeeping schedule.

"I'm Mary-Anne," the woman finally introduced herself.

"Constance." I shook her hand and glanced around. "Danny did one heck of a job with this place."

"Yes, he and Jada—" she stopped abruptly.

"Excuse me?" I said slowly.

"I'm sorry, Ms. Wells, perhaps I've—"

"Screw the official speech." I shoved her and she stumbled back. "*Jada* designed this house?"

"You can't hit me!" she hollered.

"Then you'd better start talking," I growled.

Two more women stepped into the foyer; they were dressed casually, like they hadn't been expecting anyone here.

"Come here," I snapped at them. "I want all of you to come here!"

No one moved.

"Right now!"

Then they hustled, gathering around in pajamas and sweats, and shorts, I hadn't seen a single one of these faces before. Was I actually an idiot? Hiring people I didn't even know?

"Where's Jessica, the head of this household?"

"She left." A Hispanic woman stepped forward. "Jessica turned in her resignation letter nine months ago and placed me in charge."

"Nine months ago?" I glanced around. "So ... she knew?"

No one spoke.

"Who else knew?" I asked as calmly as I could. When no

one answered, I reached for the door to stabilize myself. "You all knew that Danny and Jada built this house together?"

"Ms. Wells," the Hispanic woman continued, "I can assure you—"

"Just tell me the truth!" I screamed. I'd broken into a sweat as I clutched the door handle.

How could this be?

"This house was built for Jada." A short blonde woman stepped forward.

"What did you say?"

"Jada and I worked for the company Danny hired us from. I walked in on him and Jada one night, and they promised I'd keep my job if I remained quiet. Danny built this house so Jada could stay here, and rearranged the schedules so she'd be here when you were out."

"Ok. Thank you." Slowly, I twisted the handle to the door, swung it open, and stepped outside. "Get out. All of you."

"But, Ms. Wells, I'm new!" a woman cried.

"I said *get out*, and I won't say it again."

No one moved, and I suddenly felt something inside me snap loose.

Raging through the crowd of onlookers, I raced upstairs to find bedrooms. I ripped their clothes from the drawers, carried them to the banisters, and threw them over. Then I raced back and forth through the rooms, tearing at the drawers, throwing clothes, mirrors, perfumes—all kinds of things—as I lapsed into a screaming fit.

"Please!" A woman had made it upstairs to stop me, but I

shoved her so hard, she stumbled backwards and fell into the closet.

I ran from the room and stopped in the hall, staring at a door ahead of me. A door to a master bedroom.

With a cry of rage, I sprinted down the hall and kicked it open. Pain ricocheted up my leg, but I ignored it as I stumbled into the room and saw her name...

Jada was printed on the wall in big, bold, cursive letters. Like a child's—*no*, my blood boiled—like a *pet*. That's what she was, it's what she *is*. A little pet to him. But I don't know what's worse; being a pet or being a fool.

There were three doors in the room; one to a closet, one to the bathroom, and one that led to a small staircase which emptied directly onto the glass-enclosed walkway outside. As I stood there, I realized the walkway was for *her*. I hadn't seen another door that led to it. That was how Daniel got into this house, *unseen*, during the night. All the nights he'd spent on the toilet with a *stomachache*. All the nights he'd gone outside for some fresh air, claiming he'd stared at the stars until I'd fallen asleep. The times I was home throwing a fit in one room, he was here, having a different kind of fit.

I unraveled.

"Get out!" I screamed as I turned and ran down the stairs. "I want everyone out!"

People were moving now, grabbing things, and racing out the open door and across the lawn. Meanwhile, I let myself be consumed by my emotions. I dragged pans off the stove. Ripped food from the fridge. I broke plates against the tile floor. In a fit of rage, I pulled and pulled until the door came off the fridge. I took a mallet to the cabinets, beating them in and breaking them up, and then I beat the floor, cracking the tiles and shattering the beautiful décor.

This had all been for her. My own husband had spent my money taking care of her during our marriage. And I was the fool who let it happen.

Snatching a kitchen knife from the block, I turned in a circle, chest heaving as I thought of what I wanted to do next. I was going to cut the bed up in the master bedroom, and carve that woman's name out of the wall.

Then I heard Keesha's voice.

"Constance!"

I stopped immediately.

"Connie?" Keesha said slowly, and I turned to find her and Viv standing in the kitchen entrance. One last housekeeper pushed by Viv in a rush to escape, Viv didn't even react. That's when I knew how bad I looked—how bad this all looked.

Clothes were everywhere, broken plates and glass were strewn throughout the room, the house was in complete chaos.

"Connie, baby," Keesha stepped closer, "I need you to put the knife down."

"H-Her name," I could barely speak, "her name is on th- the wall upstairs."

I saw Viv's expression turn from fear to anger to pity.

Keesha stepped a little closer. "Baby girl, you know I'll handle it. But just put the knife down."

I wondered what I looked like to them. My clothes had

gotten stained from containers of food bursting open as I'd thrown them around. My hair was wild and tangled, my makeup smudged. I was holding a butcher knife, shaking and undoubtedly disheveled. If Jada or Danny had been there, I might've killed one of them.

"Ms. Wells…" Vivian didn't always call me that. Only when she was being formal. "You can trust us, remember? We're your friends."

"I trusted *him*," I whispered shakily. "He was my husband."

"Connie, I know you're angry, but I just need you to lower the knife and then we can talk about it."

"I don't want to talk!" I screamed. "I don't want to talk! *He* never talked! And I was so stupid!"

"No." Keesha shook her head as she took another step forward. "Connie, you weren't stupid, you were betrayed. Have I ever betrayed you? Has Viv?" She tried to produce a smile, but I could tell Keesha was hurting just from seeing me like this. "It's me, Kiki. Ya home girl, ya bestie." Her voice clenched at the end of her statement, and I felt my heart hammering in anger. I was so furious, so hurt, but with trembling hands, I dropped the knife. And like good friends, they rushed to hold me.

… * …

"Connie!" Keesha hollered from the bottom of the stairs.

I rolled my eyes, setting my Bible and notebook down. I've

been in serious spiritual rehab over the last three weeks. I've even summoned the strength to go to both services on Sunday, *and* Wednesday night Bible study. I just needed to be fully submerged in God's presence as much as possible after finding out that Daniel had left me for 'the help.'

Those are his words, not mine.

Danny used to always call our housekeepers 'the help,' and would say cruel things about them. But now I see why. He was just trying to throw me off, trying to keep me from realizing that said 'help' was being very helpful in very many ways.

It wasn't fair, nothing that'd happened to me was fair. I wanted to blame God, to shout at Him, but what good would that do? Daniel was still gone, Jada was still pregnant, and I was still the fool who let it all happen in her own home.

Keesha called me one more time. "Constance!"

With a huff, I dragged my feet from the bed and stepped into the hall. "What?"

"Come here!"

"No."

"Please!"

"Keesha, just bring it up."

She sighed. "When are you coming out of that room?"

Now I sighed too. After that spark of madness, I holed myself up in a guest room because I didn't want to be in my own bedroom anymore. I didn't want to be where Danny had fooled me. And I didn't want to see anyone.

If I wasn't at church, I was in my room, and someone— *Keesha*—left food for me to eat. She was here to check on me now, and I know she's my best friend, but I just needed space. She's been nothing but wonderful to me, and I want to make it up to her. But I just can't right now.

"Constance, I really need you to come down here," she said.

"Why?"

"Because I planned a surprise to try to get you out of your room, and you're making it very difficult for me to give it to you."

I glanced back at my Bible and notebook on the bed and exhaled heavily. This would be the first time I left the room today for anything outside of bathroom trips. I didn't want to go, but Keesha had officially seen me at my absolute worst. I knew she wouldn't disturb me if it wasn't worth it.

Tiptoeing down the hall, I thought my heart might fail me. I could scream and turn back, and claim my anxiety had reached a boiling point, but when I peeked over the banister and saw Kiki standing there with big pleading eyes, I gave in.

One step at a time, I carried myself to the bottom of the stairs. I didn't want to go, but Keesha was very good at surprises, so I can admit I was a little curious.

"What is it, Kee?" I asked, almost cautiously.

She raised a blindfold, and I immediately took a step back, but she caught my hand still holding the railing and stepped forward. "Kee—" I protested.

"Have I ever done anything to hurt you?"

She'd been the only person in the world who'd been by my side all this time—besides Viv, but her loyalty was technically because of her job, since she was my secretary. Since high school, Keesha and I have been close. It was a typical story. Pretty girl with an okay-looking best friend, *I* was the okay-looking one, by the way. But Kee was genuine, she was kind, and I think that's why everyone loved her. From high school to college to today, Keesha has always been the one standing by my side when the dust settled.

I took a breath and stepped down another stair. The last thing I saw before she blindfolded me was her smile.

Being led through my own house with a blindfold on made the place feel like a maze. I had no idea where Keesha was taking me. My house had guest rooms, luxury bathrooms, a library, two offices, two master bedrooms, recreational rooms, a gym, and whatever else we could fit into our open floor plan. I designed it all myself. Bought a few acres of land, placed my home in the center and used the rest of the space for grasslands, parking, and apparently a house for my husband's mistress.

"Alright," Keesha said as I heard a door open in front of us, "we're about to—" she stopped walking and I bumped into her with my blindfold on.

"Kee? What's wrong?"

She released a loud sigh, then her voice came out in an edgy whisper. "He ruined the surprise, but I can't even be mad. He's exhausted."

"Who?" I reached up and yanked the blindfold off and glanced around.

I was standing in a room with taupe walls, a grey wooden

dresser with a matching chest, a large white bed, and taupe-colored blankets. There was plastic all over the floor, paint cans open, and a boy in the bed, paintbrush in hand. He was snoring and hanging over the edge of the bed. He looked like he'd flopped down after finishing his work and fell asleep without even knowing.

"Keem?" I shot a look at Keesha who just shrugged. "What is he doing here?"

"He did all this for you." She waved a hand around. "Fixed the kitchen, changed the floors, reinstalled the cabinets, and even gave this room a total makeover."

"Where..." I turned in a circle. "What room are we in?"

"The housekeepers' place."

"What?" The word came out as a whisper, not a screech.

I didn't feel angry, just a little annoyed. But I think the anger was being eaten away by the awe I felt at how unrecognizable this place was. I promised myself I'd never set foot in this house again. I'd have it torn down completely. Leveled. And I wanted to pour acid on the ground so nothing would ever grow or live in this area again.

"Keesha ... why'd you do this? You know I wanted to get rid of this place. It's his mistress's house."

"It was the *housekeepers'* home." She held her hands up defensively. "But the place was so nice; I wanted you to give it a chance before completely tearing it down. And if you don't like it, then fine."

Shaking my head, I walked to the bed and stared at Keem, sleeping quietly across it. "I can't get rid of it now. Look at all the work he's done."

"He did it all for free, too." Keesha crossed her arms. "I bumped into him on my way into this little café I was going to for lunch. He was there asking for a job application. We ended up talking and I offered him some money if he could fix the place up." She pressed her lips together, almost regretfully. "He wouldn't take a dime when I told him what'd happened."

"You *told* him?" I snapped, though I kept my voice at a whisper so I wouldn't wake Keem.

"I had to tell him. If I didn't, he would've come here and confronted you."

I pressed my palm into my forehead and sighed. "What's wrong with me? I should be angry, furious that I'm here. But I'm not."

Keesha shrugged. "Maybe you just needed to see something else."

"This was *their* place, Kee. This was where they slept together right under my nose, and I'm standing here in awe of the change."

"Maybe *you've* changed and that's why you're in awe. Maybe you've forgiven him and moved on. Maybe it doesn't hurt so bad anymore because you've been healing all this time."

I looked back at Joaquin on the bed. I had to admit, the room looked nice, and Jada's name was gone, and the entire orientation of the room was different now. I didn't even know where I was when I removed the blindfold. Change is good, but a transformation is better. I don't think I'll ever feel comfortable here, but maybe Keesha was right. Maybe I was moving on, forgiving Daniel, and just bettering myself.

"Or maybe," Keesha went on, "you're not looking out the same old window anymore. Maybe you're looking at something else."

I didn't speak for a long time. Neither did Kee. We just stood there, watching Keem sleep quietly.

"Maybe you're right," I finally whispered.

Eventually, Keesha left the room, but I stayed there a little while longer, enjoying the silence. Enjoying the peace.

15

Joaquín

I opened my eyes. My hand felt funny, and there was pain shooting through my wrist. I sat up slowly and realized I was still clutching a paintbrush, and the room was still a mess.

"Shoot," I whispered, "I was supposed to—"

"Morning."

Constance startled me as she stood in the doorway between the room and the little passageway that led back to her house. She was holding a mug of coffee; I could tell it was strong because I could smell it even from my distance. The aroma alone dragged the sleepiness out of me and gave me a boost of energy.

"Constance," I rasped in my morning voice, "Look, I fell asleep here, but I'm not a squatter. And I'm not spying on you. Keesha told me—"

"I know," she cut me off. "Kee told me you're out of your father's house and now you're couch surfing."

"She told you," I grunted, then I angrily tossed the

paintbrush into the bucket beside the bed.

"She also told me you're in need of another job, Keem. And a place to stay."

"Anything else? Did she give you my social security number too?"

Connie laughed as she hesitantly stepped into the room.

"You don't have to come in here." I stood quickly and crossed the floor to her. She stopped abruptly, and the coffee in her mug swirled the rim, almost spilling.

"I'm alright," she said, extending the coffee to me.

"Oh," I took it, "thanks."

"You're a man, right?"

I raised an eyebrow at the question, but Connie just smiled in reply. Even though it was a shy one, she looked incredible wearing it. She also had on an apricot sundress, and her curly hair had been straightened today and pulled into a ponytail. I was going to compliment her when I realized my masculinity was still hanging in the air.

Taking a big sip of the burning hot sludge, I gulped it down with a nod. "Yes, ma'am. I am a man."

She laughed. "Good. Because I have a job, but it requires a male."

I squinted. "A job that requires a *male*?"

She nodded and stepped back. "I need a chef."

"A *chef*? How's that a man's job? *Anyone* could be a chef."

"True, but I need a special chef. The kind that's well-versed in other cultures and languages. Particularly Spanish, Portuguese, and English."

I smirked and took a step closer to her. "Are you interested in a chef who knows French, and is learning Italian and Japanese?"

Her eyes were suddenly daring, and the coy smile on her perfect lips made me want to throw the coffee and scoop her up.

"I'm very interested," she told me, grinning.

"Then we may have a deal."

"There are terms." She raised her chin and bumped me with her hip as she walked by.

Sipping my coffee, I slowly turned to watch her hips sway as she moved across the room. I couldn't help but tuck my lip between my teeth—it was all I could do to resist the urge to follow her across the room.

Constance had been the only woman in a very long time to turn me into the hormonal teenager I never got to be in high school. He was still there, buried under layers of scriptures I was always packing on. But secretly, the only reason I'd never really gotten rid of him was because I hadn't known he was there until I met Constance.

Now, I'm addicted to the way it feels to be around her.

"There are three terms." She turned to face me now with three fingers raised. I shrugged, and she went on. "Term number one, you have to stay in this guest house."

"Wait, what?"

"Term number two," she continued without missing a beat.

Suddenly, I was beginning to understand what this was all

about. Connie was too shy to outright offer me the place. But that didn't bother me because I hadn't ever expected her to offer in the first place. I'd fixed it up because I hated what Danny had done to her, emotionally, mentally, even spiritually.

I just wanted to help.

"You have to cook enough food for every meal for five. Me, you, Keesha, Vivian, and her boyfriend. It'll likely just be you and me most nights but be prepared in case someone comes over."

"Me and you at night?" I raised a brow. "Everything sounds good so far, Candy."

She gasped.

"I meant Connie."

A cherry red blush burned her cheeks and she looked away, voice coming out shyly now. "The third term... You cannot visit the house after ten o'clock at night."

I felt myself blushing too, thinking of the dumb teenager inside trying to set loose. Another man might've been insulted by her term, but I only felt embarrassed because I knew how badly it needed to be in place.

I liked Connie—a lot. And I was sure she liked me. Two single Christians with this level of heat between them did not need to test their limits by allowing late night visits.

But I just needed to know...

With a calming breath, I set my coffee mug down on the bedside table and strolled to Constance. I watched her shrink before me as I asked, "What happens if I come over after ten?"

She looked nervous now—I loved the way she looked

when she wasn't sure what to say. Her eyes were naturally alluring, but when she was nervous, they were suddenly big puppy dog eyes pleading for a break. Constance had worked and rewired me, but I loved every bit of it. I was enamored with her, fascinated even. When I'm away, I can't stop thinking about her. When I'm here, I can't stop staring at her.

"If you're there after ten," she stopped as I leaned my arm against the wall beside her, letting her small frame shrink even more.

"Then what?" I challenged.

She blinked at me and then shoved me back a step. "Just don't be there!" she yelled as she stormed to the other side of the room.

"Connie, wait." I chuckled and jogged over to her. "Thank you, honestly. I don't know how to repay you, but I promise to follow all your terms, and to be gone by ten."

She eyed me before grabbing the door and opening it. "No, Keem. I should be thanking you."

... * ...

It took me about a full week to move into my new place. I had to gather all my things from the houses of my friends who'd let me sleep on their couch for the last few weeks. Constance had been really cool about my first week of work, considering I was still working at The Palace too, though now, I didn't have to pick up as many shifts.

I was happy Connie let me move into her housekeeping

home, but I was a little sullen about being taken care of by her. For now, it couldn't be helped. But once I secured a better paying job, I'd get my own place and get out of there.

I hadn't been using Connie's cars, even though she's been urging me to. I was used to walking, so it wasn't a big deal, however, I also didn't want her to give me anything else. I preferred to work for everything I had, it meant more to me that way. I knew Constance was just being nice, but she was way *too* nice. So nice that I almost broke her ten o'clock post meridian rule. But I've been good about that term, for the sake of my faith.

I didn't have much to gather from my friends' houses, but I'd been dragging my feet about returning home. I had some clothes and a few essentials I wanted to grab from the house, but I didn't know if my dad would let me in.

I left three days before the move out date he'd given me with a few boxes. A friend of mine let me borrow his car, and I was able to bring some things from the house. But I couldn't grab everything, and I knew I'd have to return at some point. I just really wish I didn't need to.

I stood at the bottom of the stairs and sighed. The longer I stood out there, the longer it would be before I faced my father. I wasn't afraid of him, but it was better to avoid him. Returning now might give him the wrong impression. He might think I'm returning with my tail tucked. Even if my tail had been chopped off, I wouldn't return. It wasn't a matter of pride or rebellion, especially since this home was where my mother had raised me, and where she'd left me. But, with the alcohol and the bitterness, the disrespect and mistreatment by my father, I preferred not to return if I didn't need to.

"I'll come back another day," I decided as I turned and left for my new home.

When I got in, I really didn't have time for much besides a shower and heating up some leftovers. Connie caught me in the kitchen scarfing down some food before work, and she took a seat on a stool.

"Hi," I said around my mouthful of food.

She giggled. "I feel like I'm seeing less of you now."

"Sorry. It's been crazy at work, plus, moving and catching up with everyone."

Constance nodded, though there was an air of loneliness surrounding her.

"I'm sorry I've been so busy," I blurted, feeling guilty.

"Oh no," she perked up and waved a hand, "friendship was not in the terms."

I laughed. "Because it was assumed that we were more than that." I leaned forward to joke with her, but her eyes shot to the countertop in shame, and I quickly backed off. Too much too soon, I guess.

"I just came to tell you that you can use the walkway instead of crossing the field when you come over."

She stood abruptly and I called out to her, "Wait, Constance. I'm sorry. I was just messing around."

She nodded but turned away to the hall. I took a deep breath before putting my plate into the sink. Maybe Connie hadn't fully sorted out her feelings for Danny, or maybe for me. I wasn't sure, she was hard to read. But I decided to stop messing with her and keep things as plain as possible unless she initiated it.

Slugging my pack over my shoulder, I headed out the front door for my shift at The Palace. Every shift, the ride to work seemed to get shorter. Or maybe I'd really gotten used to living in the middle of nowhere.

"How's the cushy life?" Kenny joked as I threw my lanyard around my neck and started toward the locker room at The Palace.

Kenny had been a good friend since I got hired here. He showed me the ropes, taught me so much about valet parking. How to spot a sucker, and how to spot someone who'd be hard pressed to give you a tip. Tips were the best part of the job. These fat cats have tons of money, and they think their money gives them power—they think it means they own the world. So they throw tips at us, I guess as some subliminal way of saying they own us.

I hate their attitudes, but I don't complain too much. They're all convinced money can buy anything, so why not take advantage of that? Of course, money really doesn't buy everything, but it's certainly persuaded me more times than my pride will allow me to admit. The bigger the tip, the better the spot I picked out for the driver.

"I'm not living the cushy life." I laughed. "It's just a place to stay until I get my own place."

Kenny wasn't buying it. After seeing Connie and I show

up at The Palace together, he's been listening to my stories about her, getting juicy gossip, even offering wayward advice. I didn't mind since I really had no one else to talk about Constance with.

"Next thing I know, she's got a ring on her finger, and a baby in her belly!" He leaned back, laughing harder than he had any right to. I waved a hand at him as we walked through the back halls of The Palace and emerged from the employee doors to find our spots in the valet section of the lot.

Two cars pulled onto the runway. A schedule of big-name clients was usually posted in our locker room with a reminder for us to look out for them and leave spaces open, but I felt sure there hadn't been anyone important scheduled for another hour. Anyone else who showed up would be placed in one of the nearby lots. They were still decent spots, but they had a longer wait time to retrieve the car, which sometimes made patrons upset.

I walked over to the car on the runway, presenting the best smile I could as I tried to ignore Kenny's wild laughter in the background. "Good evening, sir," I said as the driver rolled his window down.

"Evening." He reached into his breast pocket and pulled out a wad of cash.

I watched him count it, trying to impress me. I resisted the urge to roll my eyes. If he wasn't going to give me the whole wad, then I wasn't impressed.

The car behind him inched closer, a sleek Porsche with a bald dark-skinned man in the driver's seat, and a woman in the passenger seat. I gave him a firm nod before turning back to the schmuck counting my tip. He Adjusted his square glasses, and after all that showy money counting, he passed me a single fifty-dollar bill. That might sound like a lot, but there were nights when veterans like Kenny walked away with a tip *ten* times that amount.

I took the money, trying to remember how many spaces we had open in the nearby lot. "I'll see what I can do—"

The blaring of the car horn behind us snatched my attention from the client in front of me. I stepped forward, ready to make amends with the antsy patron, even though he hadn't been waiting more than sixty seconds. But my patience went out the window when I recognized the man in the car.

Daniel James.

He was the culprit behind Constance's downward spiral. I took a step forward, trying to make sure I was seeing clearly. I hadn't seen Daniel since the day I dragged Connie away a month or so ago. So much had happened since then. My dad put me out, Connie had more than one breakdown, I fought with myself not to remember my mother. But Daniel James hadn't batted a lash in the last month. He'd happily hurled insults at Connie, breaking her down even further. The sight of him set an old burning fire in my chest. One I'd tried to snuff out long ago.

The streets hardened me, the lack of everything froze me to my core, and the grieving made me hungry for revenge. God had intervened and had whisked away all the thoughts of retaliation and resentment about my mother's death. I'd blamed everyone. Myself, my father, which strained our relationship, the hospital, anyone in sight was to blame for the loss of my mother. But the arms of my church family held me and loved me in her absence. They showed me that God's love is all powerful and comforting and I was able to overcome the grieving. However, I *had* grieved, and it had left me with crusted scabs that never went away. And lately, those scabs were itching but not for the reasons I thought they'd be.

I had a scratch I couldn't itch because there was an undeniable correlation lingering between my mother and Constance that stiffened me at the sight of Danny. Someone had hurt both people I cared for, but I could only get vengeance on one of them, so he might end up paying for both.

Daniel raised his head when he recognized me. An icy glare—an exchange of insults—happened in our silent showdown. I could hardly get the other guy through the line and pass his keys off to Kenny before waving for Danny to pull up. It took every bit of my strength not to fly off at him.

Connie had suffered so much at his hand, and I just wanted to protect her from that. I wanted to right his wrongs; maybe because I couldn't right the wrong of the cancer that stole my mother. I couldn't protect her from the man-eating monster within her, growing rapidly off her pain.

Danny had been Constance's cancer. He'd eaten away at her, barely leaving anything behind except a broken woman. My mother's worth had never been in question as her life hung in the air. And, to me, Constance's worth had never been a question either, but it's not always about the one watching from the outside.

Constance was having trouble finding her *own* worth, and that's the deadliest kind of cancer. That's the kind that eats the slowest, enjoying every bite as it surrenders your mind to a plague, and eventually your body follows with suicide or a life of depression and recklessness.

I took a deep breath and leaned over as Daniel rolled down his window. "Good evening," I managed.

Jada sat beside Dan. She was an ugly woman. I don't mean physically; I was barely looking at her. Her attitude, her demeanor. Everything about her was ugly. She was trashy. Stealing another woman's husband, stealing a spouse was the lowest blow you could deal to a person.

"Valet boy," Danny said whimsically. "How are you, kid?"

"My name's Joaquin. How can I help you?"

"Come on, kid," he leaned out the window, "she's as good as she looks, isn't she?"

I blinked away and focused on checking my watch, trying to ignore his taunting. "What can I do for you?"

He laughed. "I don't know what sob story my ex has told you, but that woman is a box of rocks. She was my second in command by *default*. She's not good at her job. She's just another pretty face with nothing to offer a man."

I took a breath, but he noticed my rigidness and played on it.

"You bothered, boy?"

I swallowed and glanced around for help, but I'd sent Kenny off to park that other car, and there was only one more car in line. There were a few cameramen and journalists lined up, waiting for celebrities to arrive, but since no one important had showed up yet, there weren't many people there. Not that it mattered since Ken's the only one who could've helped.

"If you're not dining at The Palace tonight, I'll need you to move along," I said calmly.

He huffed. "You know what, you *have* ruined my appetite."

"But you promised, baby," Jada whined, grabbing his arm, and leaning on him. He visibly softened at her icky touch.

I snorted to myself, *it's just a matter of time until he does the same thing to her.*

"What's so funny?" Danny asked with a raised brow.

"Nothing, sir. Are you paying cash or credit?"

He frowned. "I don't pay a dime. I've given this place all my money."

"I'm sorry, sir, but if you don't—"

He cut me off with a bark of laughter. "All the money we've poured into this restaurant? I basically *own* The Palace."

We? I thought.

"Listen, my lovely fiancée is hungry and pregnant so I'm going to need you to take my keys and let me go inside." Daniel adjusted in the seat, unbuckling his belt, and getting ready to get out. Like I should just oblige him because he's Daniel James.

"You think you should always get what you want," I said.

"Excuse me?" He looked genuinely confused. "Kid, I know you feel for her but I'm telling you," he leaned out the window and whispered with a grin, "when the sex wears off and the nagging begins, you'll be done with her. She's good in bed, I can give her that, but she's useless in every other aspect."

"You don't know her," I snapped quickly.

"No, *you* don't know her. One month and you're her hero? She must've turned you out quick. That's all she's got." He blew air through his lips and pointed to his head. "Nothing goes on in there for her."

I felt blood rushing to my head, but I tried to stay calm, taking a deep breath. He wouldn't stop. He kept going on and on about how she's nothing. How stupid she was. How much better he was than her. It was ridiculous to listen to. To watch a man belittle a woman he'd been married to for five years before divorcing her for no real reason.

"You broke her," I muttered.

"What?" Daniel glanced at Jada whose shoulders were bobbing as she covered her mouth to laugh quietly. When he looked back at me with a grin, I clenched my fist and tried to stay calm.

"I didn't break Constance." He laughed… he *laughed* at her like none of this mattered. "That woman has always been broken. I just finished her off—"

I jammed my fist through the open window, enjoying the hiss of pain he let go of when my knuckles connected to his face. His head snapped back, and Jada let out a piercing cry in response. I could see her scrambling for the door when I reached inside and snatched a dazed Danny by his jacket. Yanking him forward, I punched him over and over while I tried to drag him through the window at the same time.

We twisted and riled until he got his arm out the window and managed to punch me in the gut. I held him tight, slugging him with everything I had, but Daniel didn't give up. With his arm free, he gave me a few more good punches to the ribs before I had to step back or risk him breaking my bones. Then, the car door flew open, and he stepped out.

Daniel's first punch was sloppy. I dodged it easily, but not the second. He landed a heavy fist against my face, sending me crashing to the ground. Danny was as strong as I figured he'd be, but he was also as slow as I figured he'd be.

I took a slow breath, sitting on the hard ground as Daniel rolled his sleeves up and walked over to me. I hated the sight of him. Looking down at me. Pushing up his sleeves like a father ready to discipline his child. I was not a child, and I had a father. A father I'd already tussled with. If I didn't hold back on him, I certainly wasn't going to let this guy toss me around either.

Once he was close enough, I slammed my foot into Daniel's knee. He cried out and fell forward—I was on him in seconds. We exchanged blows, body work, face beatings, we thrashed until someone finally jumped in behind me and dragged me off him.

His foot met my ribs with a brutal kick as I was being pulled away. It was so much force it knocked me over and took down the guy who'd been pulling me back. I rolled over in pain, convinced the fight was over, but then I felt a foot stomp on my side, and I let out a shout of raw pain.

Danny kicked me over and then snatched me up to my

feet by my collar. In a daze, I felt him hit me twice in the ribs again and I knew he'd probably cracked one. I hollered as he hit me, but it was mostly a reflex. I'd sustained three cracked ribs in a different fight a few years ago, I could handle this.

His arm swung back for another punch, but I ducked and shoved my fist into his chest. He squealed and took a breath, stumbling backwards before I took all my anger and let it rush into my fist, landing a crunching blow to his face. There was an audible snapping noise, louder than the screaming and wailing and clicking of cameras behind us. Danny went limp under the pressure of my fist. His eyes rolled to the back of his head, and he fell backwards into the grass.

I didn't kill him. I'd just knocked him out. But now Mr. Adams was outside yelling at me to get into his office. I grunted, casting one more look at Daniel as he lay on the ground in his shiny silver suit. I stopped walking when I saw Jada standing near the entrance with her mouth covered. She was standing across the way, watching from a distance. Like she always had.

"Does he even mean something to you?" I asked quietly.

She looked at me, brows packed together as she snarled, "What do you think?" Her voice didn't shake, her hands weren't trembling. Jada was getting tired of Daniel already.

I shook my head. "All of this for what?"

"Joaquin! Get inside!" Mr. Adams looked like a flame, blazing a trail through the crowd as he marched ahead of me. Turning away, I didn't look at Jada again as I rushed inside to Mr. Adams' office.

Mr. Adams slammed the door and paced back and forth. I watched him for a second before I sighed.

He stopped pacing. "Are you… *sighing*? Is this a game to you?"

"No, sir."

"Don't '*no, sir*' me! You just got rid of the one person single-handedly holding The Palace together! Now I've got to shoestring and bubblegum things together and hope it all works out!"

"Mr. Adams, I think—"

"*I think I've heard enough*," his voice was dangerously quiet. "Pack your things," he said as he moved behind his desk.

"But, sir!" I licked my lip, and the taste of blood made my stomach feel even worse. "You didn't hear what he said. He was antagonizing me!"

"I don't care if he was *choking* you! You just put us in the worst possible position. When he wakes up and remembers everything that happened, his funding will stop, and The Palace may go under."

So, he wasn't lying, I thought, *he really didn't have to pay.* I had no idea he hadn't been lying out there—or at least *exaggerating*—since I thought the only reason he didn't pay when I first met him was because his name was on the complimentary valet list when he came a month ago with Jada.

"I've tried to protect you for old time's sake, but Keem, you've given me no choice."

I sat back in my seat and stared at nothing. "You know I'm a hard worker, Mr. Adams. You just hope my absence appeases

Daniel."

"Don't make this personal," he snapped.

"What am I *supposed* to make it?"

"You're supposed to be a man and acknowledge that you were wrong here!"

"Am I wrong, or was my father wrong?"

"Keem—"

I stood and moved toward the door.

"Keem!"

"My father told me once about a friend who wouldn't help him, after everything he'd done for him; lied, cheated." I glared at him. "The only thing his friend said to him was that he needed to be a man and acknowledge his wrongdoing. That was ironic because my father was only in a bad position because his friend pulled the rug from under his feet when a drug operation went wrong."

Mr. Adams sank into his desk, glancing away now that his anger had suddenly tamed.

"When my mom got sick, Dad needed some money," I continued, "but that friend wouldn't help him. And then he gave his son a job out of pity. But I was the idiot who rode off those fumes for too long." I turned and grasped the doorknob, only looking back to nod at Mr. Adams. "Goodnight, sir."

16

Joaquín

I took the back door, avoiding Constance. I couldn't let her see me like this. I didn't want her to know that I got into a fight with Danny *and* lost my job all in one night. I wasn't stupid, I knew she would eventually find out, but just for tonight, I needed time to think. Alone.

As soon as I entered my new home, I tossed my keys onto the counter and headed up the stairs. Each step made me groan in agony, as every breath felt like someone dragging a fishhook through my lungs. Danny had cracked me across the face a few good times, but he'd punched me more times in my ribs like we were boxing and not squaring off. The adrenaline kept me from feeling most of it but getting to the top of the stairs winded me like I had never taken a flight of stairs before. I knew something was wrong, most likely a fractured rib, or at least some bad bruising. Danny hit hard, but I gave him all I had in exchange.

Falling against the door with a sigh, I slowly shoved it

open.

"Keem, I told you that you can take the archway. Why didn't you..." Connie's words trailed off as I looked up from the door. I hadn't even noticed the lamp was on by my bedside until it was too late. I should've seen that from outside the door, but I was just so tired and so unfocused. Plus, I hadn't expected her to be here. But there she was sitting on my bed, hands folded like she'd been waiting for me.

"Keem?" She frowned.

I dropped my head and turned to leave.

"Where are you going?"

Honestly, nowhere, because I didn't really want to take those stairs again. Maybe I'd just sleep in one of those guest rooms. This house was huge.

"Keem—"

"Listen, Connie, I'm tired," I said sharply. "I just want to get to bed."

"What's wrong?" she prodded, not letting it go.

I shook my head. "Constance, *please*." I didn't want her to see me like this.

"Why won't you look at me?"

I didn't speak.

"Look at me, Keem."

"No."

"Keem..."

"I said no!"

"Joaquin!"

"What!?" I snapped my vision up to her. "Is this what you

wanted to see? You wanted to see me with bruises and a black eye?"

She covered her mouth as she stood from the bed and crossed the floor. "Keem, what happened?"

I glanced away. "Nothing."

"Please..." Her warmth was radiating against me as she stood close. "Keem, I just want to help you."

I sighed, dropping my shoulders. "I got into a fight at work."

"Why? With whom?"

I couldn't say it, but I didn't need to. In the thick silence, our eyes met, and she knew... She *knew*.

Connie shook her head. "No..." She started backing away from me. "*Danny* did this to you? Y-You *fought* him?"

"You didn't hear what he said about you, Connie." I stepped toward her, forgetting the pain throbbing through my body. She'd backed away, but I knew she wasn't backing away because of me, she was shocked, and I could see that shock on her face as she dropped her gaze to the floor. She couldn't look me in the eye, not even as she spoke.

"Keem, you don't have to protect me. You shouldn't have done this."

"I couldn't stand by and let him say those things." I tried not to snap at her, but it felt like Constance was protecting him now, and my heart began to break. "He was saying things, *laughing* at how broken you are. He thinks it's a joke."

"Keem," she said quietly, but I waved her off.

"You don't care. You don't care at all, Connie. You're

worried about him after I lost my *job* for you!"

"That's not true!"

"Yes, it is," I grumbled as I marched past her into the room. I pressed my hands to the wall, the pain resurfacing as reality settled on me. How could she be angry when I *protected* her?

"How dare you?" she said behind me. "After what he's done to me, you would assume I'm angry over *him*? I thought you knew me better than that."

I pushed off the wall and turned to face her. She was still standing by the door, hand squeezing her oversized sweatshirt as she fought the trembling in her voice.

"I don't know anymore, Connie. One minute I can barely breathe because you're smiling at me, and the next minute you're cold and telling all your friends that I mean nothing to you."

She jerked back. "Is that what this is about? Proving that you mean something to me? So, you start a fight with someone?"

"Are you kidding me?" That was it. I'd reached my breaking point with her. Before I knew it, I was shouting at her, throat raw with anger. "I *defended* you! I didn't start a fight to get your attention, and I'm glad I didn't since it only put your focus back on *Danny*!"

She darted across the room and shoved me hard. "You don't know what you're talking about!" She shoved me again, her hair springing with every movement. "You have no idea and you've never asked!" She shoved me again, backing me into the wall now, but her strength was gone. I could hear it in her quivering voice.

"No one ever talks to me..." she said. "They just make assumptions. They make up their own stories, and I'm left trying to figure out where these stories originated." Tears streamed down her cheeks and a small fist gently pounded against my chest at each word. "No... One... Ever..."

"Constance..."

"No." She shook her head, her fist hitting me a little harder. "You don't get to do this to me. You don't get to be angry without ever asking me. I can't do it again. I can't take the silence. I can't piece things together again."

With my anger cooling, and Connie standing there with tears on her cheeks, I could see just how broken Danny had truly left her. Constance was fighting so hard to be stronger, to stand on her own when she'd never done that before. It was hard to find your legs when you didn't know you'd had them to begin with.

Constance was learning to have faith again and to be strong, she was learning to walk all over again. Seeing someone become so broken. So pitiful. Her fight for strength should've been uplifting. But all it did was break my own heart for her and fuel my anger towards Danny. He was like a Mack truck, coming out of nowhere on the road and ramming into an animal, leaving it for dead. Miraculously though, someone came along and saved the animal, or rather, *God* came along and touched Constance.

"I'm sorry, Connie," I whispered. "I'm so sorry."

She wiped at her tears with a nod and began to back away. But I reached out and caught her wrist. "Don't go," I said quietly.

"Keem—"

"Please, Connie." I moved from the wall to embrace her, but she was stiff in my arms. "I'm sorry."

"You didn't even ask. You didn't try to understand. Why? This isn't like you."

"I know," I muttered. "I was angry. I was frustrated because I think I've been afraid that you'll always love Danny, and you'll never have room for me." She was silent, but her rigidness eased at my words. In this stifling moment, all I could do was tell her the truth. Tell her how afraid I really was of never being more than the valet kid to her.

"Is that why you did it?" she asked. "You fought him to force me to make room in my life for you? You lost everything. Why, Keem? Why would you do that?"

She wiped aggressively at her tears, and I realized just how wrong I'd been. Connie didn't tell her friends she didn't like me because she *actually* didn't like me, she denied her attraction because she was *afraid* to like me. Afraid to feel happy, to feel the things I could make her feel that Danny never did. This was all new for her; being cared about, being appreciated... being loved.

"You're worth it to me," I said. "I'd lose everything if it means I get to keep you." I pulled her against me.

"Stop," she whispered as I lowered my lips to her neck. I didn't hesitate today... I kissed her. "Let me show you," I whispered between kisses against her neck, "let me show you that I want you. That you mean everything to me."

"Keem, we can't," she whispered back, though her body betrayed her words. Her hands were racing through my hair, pulling me closer to her.

"Tell me this is what you want."

She didn't speak, and when I pushed her against the door, she gasped.

"Tell me," I whispered again.

"I... I want this."

Her words shifted me to her lips. She gasped, and I groaned. There were so many other feelings in this. The way she clung to me, the way she gasped when I'd pull away and kiss her neck. She hadn't been loved in so long, her desire leaked through her lips with every kiss and sigh.

I lifted her off her feet, the pain making me grunt, but she didn't notice. My ribs were aching as I carried her. I thought she'd stop for air and notice that my breathing was labored, but she didn't. Connie kissed me until I laid her on the bed. I needed a break, but I didn't want to take one. Apparently, she didn't either as she went for my shirt, pulling at it to get it off. I reached up to help her, but as soon as I lifted my arms, I grunted and stopped.

"What's wrong?" she whispered through heavy breathing.

"Nothing." I shook my head as I pulled my shirt off. My ribs were the problem, aching and throbbing. While the pleasure infiltrated my mind, making me forget everything, my body didn't. My body was still aching, and Connie's rounded eyes were now staring at my body.

"Keem, your ribs are bruised."

"No," I tossed my shirt to the side, "I'm fine."

My lips brushed hers and she welcomed me as I crawled onto her. Ignoring the feeling in my chest, I leaned down and began undressing Constance. She was a little shy, but she had no reason to be. The oversized shirt came off quicker with her help since I couldn't move my right arm that well or I'd make my ribs ache worse. I played it cool, and she didn't notice.

Beneath me, Constance looked like every bit of the woman she'd told me she was. I never doubted her, but looking at her full figure, her smooth chocolate skin, I couldn't resist her any longer. Slipping a finger beneath her bra strap, my heart thudded so loudly, I know she heard it. I was about to have my first sexual experience... with Constance Wells. She was a woman you read about in magazines, literally. Rich, sexy, business owner, black. She had everything, and in a few moments, she'd have my first for a lot of things too.

There was a pang of guilt in the back of my head. Like if I could sift through my thoughts of lust right now, I'd find my reason for the guilt. But honestly, I didn't want to acknowledge Him. I wanted this even though I knew it was wrong.

Was I really going to do this? How do I stop when I'm this far in?

Constance was pulling me toward her for another kiss, and when I drew back, all faithful thoughts were gone.

I was tugging at her bra again. My eyes reached hers for permission in the thick silence. She'd come a long way since

Danny, but this was going to be a *really* long way. I wanted her to be okay with this, I *needed* her to be. Her hand reached my face, and her eyes were filled with lust as she leaned forward and kissed me. When she laid back again, I pulled on the strap, and I noticed a silver chain tucked in her chest, the pendant hidden in her cleavage. I stopped pulling on her bra strap and reached for her necklace instead... it was a crucifix.

"Oh my goodness." I let go of her necklace and moved away. But it was a sloppy aching movement, and I fell from the bed in pain.

"Keem!"

"I'm alright," I said as I felt the dizzying pain swirling inside. When Connie leaned over the edge of the bed, her cross pendant dangled over the edge too. I couldn't stop staring at it.

"We almost—"

"I know," she said, grabbing her cross. "I'm so stupid."

"It wasn't you. I shouldn't have pressured you."

"But I should have stopped you. I'm responsible for my own sins, Keem. Don't take all the blame."

I smirked as best I could as I sat up. "You couldn't resist me."

She rolled her eyes. "This isn't funny. We almost had sex."

My shoulders slumped. "I know. I'm just embarrassed. I don't really know how else to respond right now."

"I wanted to keep going," she said as she moved from the bed and sat beside me on the floor. "We can start by admitting what we felt."

I nodded, grasping her hand as she went on.

"I wanted us to have sex," Connie admitted. "And I wouldn't have called it a mistake afterward."

"Constance…" I had no idea what to say. I'd almost lost my virginity, she almost lost something too, I guess. But we came dangerously close to committing a sin.

God was expecting so much from me, and I'd ruined it. How could I ever tell my father the truth about Constance with this hanging over me? Was God still going to use me? He knew that I would fall into lust, and yet, He still prophesied that my light would draw my father back to Him.

"I'm an idiot." I dropped my face into my hands, feeling the guilt sink in.

"Stop it." Constance tugged on my arm. "You're not an idiot."

"I am." I lifted my eyes to see her looking up at me with a worried expression. Her normally smooth brown skin tensed into a frown with furrowed brows.

"Something is going on with you," she said, leaning closer. "What is it?"

"This is bad timing." I stared at her pleading lips, heart beginning to thud all over again. I swallowed thickly. "Constance … I still want to…"

"Oh…" She let go of my arm and scooted a good six feet away.

We fell into the most painfully awkward silence, but Connie was respectful, keeping her distance and giving me time to cool down. Despite the pain and the guilt, there was still that dirty little desire burning like a match in my chest. No one had put a dampener over it to suffocate it, I just hoped that it would burn out on its own. But it wouldn't and it wasn't going to because it hadn't been addressed at all. Until now.

"This isn't the first time I've felt like this about you," I said, hanging my head.

"Would it surprise you if I said the same thing?"

I looked over at Connie now, she lifted a thin shoulder and said, "Guys like women, women like men."

My brow raised. "I'm a man to you?"

She snorted. "Joaquin, this isn't about that."

I found a way to laugh too in the moment filled with tension that was finally dissipating.

"What do we do?" she asked.

"I have no idea."

"Do we just ask for forgiveness?"

"I think so, but I just feel like we should do more than that."

"Me too," she sighed.

"God wants to use me to bring my father back to Him, but I feel like I just screwed everything up."

"I don't think so. The redeemed always love God more than the ones who just follow His guidance."

I shifted to see her, making me wince in pain.

"I've been reading the Bible more." Connie smiled sheepishly. "In Luke, when that woman came inside and anointed Jesus' feet with her tears and perfume, He told Peter that those with much to be forgiven, have more to love. Those with little to be forgiven, love less."

A quiet chuckle escaped me. "I remember that story."

"I always thought it was a license to sin." She laughed. "I thought, if I screwed up a lot, then I would love God a lot. But after reading that passage carefully, I realized the true meaning was quite the opposite. This woman was broken and regretful and had so many tears, which she used to wash the feet of Jesus."

"She was *sincere*," I whispered, realizing what Connie was getting at.

"Yes. And I think that was another lesson there. It wasn't about the perfume, it wasn't about her hair, it was about a broken woman giving her all to the Master. And in turn, He forgave her. So, I don't think you're out of the race yet. I think we just have to get right with God again."

Taking a deep breath, I nodded. "You're right."

"Do you…" she paused. "Do you want to pray together?"

"You want to pray with me?"

She shrugged, turning away quickly. "It was a dumb suggestion. Prayer is very personal. Very intimate. I shouldn't—"

"You should." I slid over to her and took her hand. She stared at them for a second before looking up at me.

"Are you sure this is okay?"

I almost laughed. Lifting her hand, I kissed it. "I'm fine."

"Ok then," she said, squeezing my hand. "I guess I'll lead us in prayer."

17

Constance

I stepped out of the car and headed for the house; I'd left early this morning to see our accountant. Viv got a hold of me last night and said an old business who'd been working with Daniel had pulled out after some misunderstanding. He's giving us his business, and without even taking a meeting, he sent over a retainer of fifteen percent of his total costs up front. We'll get another other fifteen percent if we can get him the deal he wants. Vivian got me the paperwork this morning, and I talked to our accountant about the kind of ads we can manage with the new funding.

    I'd need to call Keesha this morning and get the whole team over to discuss the way we can remarket ourselves and swing this deal. I've got an idea, and I know it'll work, it's just a matter of wearing the client down sometimes. That's always been the biggest difference between Danny and me. He'd blitz, wanting the biggest deal at the fastest pace. But sometimes you can pull an extraordinary deal with more time, or at least rework the terms to get backdoor money for the client. But clients who wanted things to work out quickly—which was most clients—preferred Danny. He'd get the results they wanted in the time frame they wanted. I could've gotten them better results, but who wants legal action hanging over your head for too long?

"We're not competing anymore," I whispered as I walked through the door. Kicking my heels off right there, I marched up the winding stairs to my real bedroom.

The guest bedroom had served me well until I almost serviced myself with Keem last night. The memories sent a cool sweat down my back, and I flopped onto the king bed. All morning, I was distracted with thoughts of Keem and our night together. The whole night and day thing freaks me out, but in that weird kinky way. It's like, one minute he's just a kid, trying to figure things out in this world. But the next second, he's a man, forcing my hips against him, working me for his pleasure and somehow mine too. Like he already knows what I like without even asking me.

I groaned loudly into my hands as I turned over in the bed.

I want to see him.

A glance at my watch told me it was just eight-thirty in the morning. Maybe he was still sleep or just waking up. We'd talked and prayed last night, but after prayer I decided to leave. It was awkward and we left things unsaid, though I think our actions said a lot more. Which is why I *shouldn't* go see him. I should just stay here, stay put and not think about him.

Yeah right.

I changed into a sundress, let my hair down, and waltzed down the walkway connecting my house to his place within five minutes. It was weird, feeling excited over this guy. I didn't want to admit to my feelings because he'd swooped into my life so suddenly, with no regard to what it might look like or feel like to *me*. That's what made him so youthful. He just did things. Without care. Without concern. Without the life experience to know that he *should* be concerned.

He kissed my neck, he held me close, he ran a few miles in the dead of night to see me. To wipe my tears away. And he never asked for anything in return. But I think that's what made him a man too. His qualities were synced with his desires. Keem knows what he wants, he just acts shy around me because I don't know what *I* want.

Who's the adult here? Not me, apparently. I just didn't know if it was alright to feel this way so suddenly. To no longer sob and cry over Daniel. That's what all divorcees did when they actually loved their husbands. The ones who didn't do that ran off with a new man, didn't they? That's what all the books and movies said.

I sighed as I stood at the door. There were two things that were unsettling about my divorce. Until Keem came along, I thought I'd drown in tears. But it's like he came into my life and gave me a reason to move on.

Secondly, whenever I'm with Joaquin, I feel like I'm actually happy. Happier than I've been since I met Daniel. I feel like I'm in high school with Keesha again, laughing at boys and having my first crush all over again. And that's why I'm afraid.

When was being happy a reason to be afraid?

There's always more to it, like the fact that Keem lost everything last night for me. He's defended me from the beginning, and I feel so overwhelmed every time I think about it. But the little boy within him that always reminds me of our differences yelled at me for not telling my friends that I might have feelings for him. If we hadn't been arguing, I think I would've laughed. However, Keem was serious... which just meant he was serious about *me*.

I gulped and knocked on the door. No one answered. That should've been my cue to leave, but I raised my fist and pounded twice more before taking the liberty of opening the door myself.

"Keem? You asleep? I think we should talk." I stepped inside, but the bed was empty, and the room was still dark. The blinds were pulled shut, the only light reaching into the room was crawling from beneath the bathroom door. It was pulled up, not closed. I stood by the door now—listening. I was totally eavesdropping, but I couldn't just walk inside.

Footsteps called out as he came to the door. I tried to back away, but Keem was already opening the door as I tripped backwards.

"Connie?" He frowned for a split second before snorting. "What are you doing?"

My eyes traced his frame. Joaquin Rivera was definitely not the good Christian boy I thought he was, at least not in the towel wrapped around his waist.

Water rolled down his chest as steam rose from his body. Broad shoulders that zipped down to a trimmed waist made me stare like a little girl seeing a nude man for the first time. Except Keem wasn't completely nude. His manhood was covered, but the parts of him that weren't were just as intriguing. I shamelessly stared.

"Connie," his husky morning voice called out to me, and I had to rip my eyes from his trimmed chest, and muscular arms. Daniel was a ball of buff, but Keem was nearly six foot three with v-lines screaming at me.

"I-I was just," I stopped and shook my head, "I was just coming to say we should talk, but if you want to talk later—"

"We can talk now." He shrugged nonchalantly.

"Oh." I blinked at his figure again. I could feel sorry for his bruises from last night, but somehow, they made this moment even hotter. *Something is definitely wrong with me.*

"I'll grab some clothes, but if you want to start talking, you can." Keem moved by me into the room. My eyes followed like a child's, watching as he pulled out a black shirt and held it up. The curve of his back, the way his muscles flexed with his movements and his wet curly hair were dripping down his figure, I was so tempted to have a redo of last night.

God is truly merciful and loving. Because He knew if I'd seen Keem in better light last night looking like this, there would've been sinning going on until dawn. I'm not proud of this weakness, but I am so incredibly grateful that God kept me last night.

"Right. Last night," I said, mouth suddenly dry. "I feel like we didn't really talk about what happened."

"I thought we did." Joaquin tossed the shirt on the bed and reached for some lotion.

"No, we didn't talk about *why* it happened."

"Well, what happened?"

"You know what happened."

He turned to me, a smirk on his face as he put deodorant on. "Nah, Candy, tell me what happened."

"Don't do that." I chewed my lip. "Stop it, Keem."

He bunched his shoulders. "I haven't done a thing."

"Why do you play games with me?"

He laughed, setting the stick of deodorant on the dresser before crossing the room to me. Bare shoulders moving rhythmically to taunt me with desire. "I'm not playing any games, Candy," he said softly.

The nickname right now was killing me.

"I'm serious. I told you last night, but I'll tell you again. Everything I lost was worth it if it means I get to keep you by my side." Keem looked serious. "I'll find another job, do whatever, but that only matters to me because of you."

His gaze slipped to my lips for a second and when he stepped forward, my hand immediately went to his chest.

"Joaquin."

"I'm not trying to do anything." He leaned forward, pressing his ungodly firm and chiseled chest into my palm as he kissed my cheek.

For some reason, that chaste little peck made my heart race faster than the thoughts of the previous night. I sighed, his chest still against my hand. I could see the bruising spidering out from his ribs, sending pink stripes up towards his chest and down to his hips.

"Keem, this looks serious." My hand moved to follow the red that faded into purple and blue along his ribs.

He winced and said through clenched teeth, "I'm alright."

"No, you're not."

"Connie." He grabbed my hand, yanking my vision from his bruised ribs to his bruised face. "I'm alright. I've gotten into fights before. A week and it'll be like it never happened."

"And until then, what are we supposed to do?"

"*We?*" He quirked a brow.

I tugged my hand from his. "I meant *you.*"

His grin disappeared, and his gaze became distant, like he was thinking deeply.

"What's wrong?"

"Last night, Danny said something."

"What was it?"

"He said, '*We*' put a lot of money into The Palace.' What is he talking about?"

"Oh." I shrugged. "I invested in The Palace when we first got married. I've also made hefty donations for the past few years on behalf of my business."

"Are you sure it was on behalf of the business? Because Mr. Adams said if *Daniel* pulls his funding, then The Palace will go under."

"*His* funding? No, we wrote checks from the *business* for The Palace."

"Who sent the checks?"

I closed my eyes. "Danny did."

When I opened my eyes, Keem was pulling his shirt on over his head.

"So, he cheated me out of something else."

"No." He looked up at me from his drawer. "He just put a business back into your hand."

"I don't think you get it, Keem. He took the checks, likely got rid of them, and wrote the checks out for himself and gave something to The Palace to keep them quiet. He already stole clients from me, money's no different." I exhaled a defeated sigh as I turned my back when he pulled out a pair of boxers.

"He took money from the business and invested it into his business," Keem said while I stared at the wall so he could dress in private. "Which means, technically, you own either half of The Palace, or you own half of his business. If we can get those checks in front of a judge—or even a bank statement, *anything*—then you just took back everything he's stolen from you."

I thought about it for half a second, but my mind and heart for once were on the same page. "I don't want what he stole from me."

"Constance—"

"No." I shook my head. "I will not go begging the courts to give me back what was stolen. I don't want anything from him."

"Don't let pride get in the way, Connie." Joaquin walked over to me, fully clothed, and placed a hand on each shoulder to turn me to face him. "You're still seeing it as you versus him, and it's not like that."

"You're one to talk." I stepped away from his hands, glaring up at him. There was empty confusion on his face, an expression that held no weight because he knew I was telling the truth. "Keem, you lost your job for me. Took a beating for me. You don't have to do this either. The only reason you want to fight is to get Danny back."

He set his hands on his lithe hips as he hung his head. "You don't know what it's like to *not* be stolen from."

"What?" Now I wore a confused expression.

"You have no idea what it's like to keep watching from the outside. To keep watching people you care about." He looked up. "People you *love* get everything taken from them in slow methodical tugging."

I placed my hands over my mouth, unable to speak as he went on.

"You're not my mother," he acknowledged, "but I care about you, Constance. I sat with you, heard you cry, watched you fall apart right in my own arms. I'm angry all over again, begging God every night for help, but it's so hard again. I'm trying to keep a lid on it, but Danny's like a bulldozer. Ripping a door off the hinges to let the anger back in."

"You feel like you couldn't protect your mother, and now you feel like you can't protect me," I said softly.

His voice was flat. "Yeah."

I stood there an extra moment, trying to figure out what all this meant, what everything *could* mean. But Keem was moving the next minute, grabbing things from around the room and heading for the door.

"Where are you going?"

"I just need some fresh air," he said as he stood in the doorway.

"Will you come back?"

He had a bag hanging over one shoulder, and as he turned to me, I couldn't help but notice the desperation in his eyes. "Do you want me to come back?"

"I want ... I want you to *stay*."

His bag hit the floor.

"Constance—"

"Stay with me, Keem."

He crossed the room only to stop short and stand there staring down at me. As he raised his hands and cupped my face, he looked surprised, like he couldn't believe I'd asked him to stay. Like he couldn't believe he'd agreed to.

"I'll stay, Constance, and I'll protect you."

"Okay," I whispered with a nod.

His lips pressed over mine, and for the first time in my entire life, I think I wasn't the only one who felt like they were in love.

18

Joaquín

"Connie," I called as I dried my hands on a towel. I'd made her eggs, bacon, and rye toast with freshly squeezed orange juice for breakfast. It wasn't fancy at all, nothing like I knew she was expecting, but I didn't have time this morning. I woke up late after spending all evening listening to Kenny go on about how I knocked Daniel out last week and when he came to, Danny and Mr. Adams had a screaming match. It ended with Daniel and Jada leaving and eventually, Mr. Adams started making payroll cuts.

I hadn't told anyone about the way Jada reacted to Daniel the night we fought. She was callous and her motives were clear; she enjoyed being on the arm of a billionaire—even though that arm wasn't hers to be on in the first place.

While he was still married, Jada caught Daniel's eye, and she's held onto it ever since. I read a book once where this robot fell in love with a princess. She'd 'caught his eye,' literally. He popped it out his head and gave it to her one day for safekeeping in case his files ever got corrupted. Later, when he was knocked unconscious, she had to take that eye and save his life with it. It was a very good play on the *catching one's eye* metaphor, however, there was real love between those two characters. The princess had fallen in love with a hunk of metal, treating it like a human. She was kind and loving, everything Jada wasn't. Because Jada wasn't in love with Daniel, and the night of the fight, it showed. I thought, all this time, that Daniel would be the one to betray her, but now I know it's quite the other way around.

"Connie!" I called again.

"Coming!" Connie responded.

I set out her utensils, then traded my apron for my backpack. I was going job hunting again today. I know I'm not a burden to Constance, but I'm a burden to *myself*. I'm wracking my brain everyday with the stress of Connie taking care of me.

I couldn't afford to take care of Connie as a billionaire, though I really wanted to. But my masculinity couldn't afford to be taken care of by a billionaire, so I was at a serious crossroads. The only thing to do, to keep my self-respect intact, was beat the pavement until I found another good paying job to at least tackle my *own* bills.

I had enough in savings and from my last two checks coming from The Palace to last at least eight months, since I'd saved up for four months of rent and utilities, plus a security deposit. I just never found a place in my range.

Constance walked inside wearing a spaghetti strap shirt tucked into yoga pants. Her hair was tied into a neat bun, and she was wearing a sweatband. Connie always worked out before breakfast. Squatting, running, lifting. We've got plans to exercise together, but if I'm honest, *she's* planning to workout, I'm just planning to be a hormonal teenager in a gym with his crush.

I've got to grow up.

"Good morning," she said as she sat in a highchair at her bar.

"Morning, Candy." I pushed the plate to her.

"Are you going somewhere?" She nodded at my backpack.

"Yeah."

"Oh." She glanced away.

"Something wrong? I'll be back in time to make you lunch." I chuckled. "I know you really like lunch—and dinner." That's usually when I got my fanciest.

"No, I'm not worried about that. I just didn't know you were leaving again."

I sighed. I'd been out looking for a job every day this week as opposed to last week when I still had a bruised face and ribs. I'd spent my days with Connie, exploring her house, discussing her business, and cooking, of course. We'd had fun, and we were getting used to being around each other. But I told her I wasn't comfortable being taken care of, so I had to find a job. She didn't fight me or sing along with me either. She told me that was for me to decide but she also reassured me that I could stay and not worry about anything.

Constance constantly felt like she needed to repay me. I wasn't sure how to prove to her that she didn't. That she'd already repaid me. If she just wanted to put a value on it, however, I wasn't keeping a tally of favors between us. I did everything for Connie because she meant something to me. Because I wanted to be here with her.

After rolling around in bed last week when we almost had sex, I assumed Connie felt the same. And it's possible somewhere inside she did feel the same, but she was clearly having trouble accepting my care for her as just a man caring for a woman he liked. I could understand that, considering all of our passion for each other nearly erupted in a night of lust. Connie didn't need physical intimacy right now, she needed to know that I was here for her heart. Her emotions. Her peace of mind. I cared about all of that first, having her body was just a bonus.

"Can I come with you?" she asked abruptly. It'd been silent for a few moments as I'd receded into my thoughts, but then she was speaking again.

I adjusted my bag over my shoulder. "I'm going on a few interviews. I got two call-backs, and three first interviews, so I'll be busy."

"I see." She glanced down at her plate, food relatively untouched.

"Come on, Candy, eat your eggs or they'll get cold."

She nodded.

"Constance…" I hated it when she got upset. Her pout was to die for. "I'll probably be done around three. I can come back, make you lunch, and then we can go to my dad's house. There are a few things I was planning to pick up from there this week."

"Really?" She perked up.

"Maybe we won't get into a fight if you're there," I joked.

She only gave me a half smile.

"Well, I've got to get going, but I'll see you when I get back."

She nodded and started in on her food, munching her bacon like a happy child. I leaned across the counter and kissed her forehead before leaving.

... * ...

I didn't think anything through. Unfortunately, I realized my mistake after it was already too late. I was standing on my father's porch with him blinking at me and then at Constance who was totally overdressed. I was used to seeing her in her casual long skirts and blouses, but to my father, and everyone else from my neighborhood, my little candy cane stuck out like it was the dead of March with Christmas nowhere in sight.

"Hey, Dad—"

"How dare you bring her to my house?" he seethed.

"Dad, I can explain."

"Go ahead." He crossed his fat little arms and his scowl deepened.

"May I explain?" Constance raised her hand.

My father was too baffled to even speak. He stared at the woman responsible for 'taking' the last bit of my mother from him. But she was unafraid and unshaken. Though my father's scowling face was intimidating to *me*, Constance was used to dealing with men and their bruised egos. The only man Connie had never stood up to, or rather, stood *toe to toe* with was Danny. She never expected to have to stand up for herself against her own husband, but now she was getting stronger, and I was sure if the time ever came, Connie could stand up to him too.

"My name's Constance Wells. Your son and I—"

"I know who you are," my father nearly snapped.

Connie's hand was extended, but after his aggression, she lowered her hand with a nod. "Then you should know that your son is in good hands."

"My son is being taken care of by a *woman*." He leaned back and let out a laugh that made his belly jump beneath his sweat stained shirt.

Connie gave me a flat smile before she returned her attention to my father. She wasn't apologetic or even shaken, Connie looked like she couldn't care less what my father made of our situation.

"Dad," I interrupted his laughter, "Connie's just letting me stay with her for a while."

"What is there to be ashamed of? What is there to defend?" Constance looked at me. "You helped me, defended me, brought my faith back, and now I owe you. Paying off your mother's debt was just a down payment on what I owe you. Having my faith restored," she looked away, down at her hands as they clasped together, "I can never truly repay you for that."

"*Faith*," my father's words were slurred for a moment, and

I knew he wasn't talking about belief in God, he was talking about my mother, Faith Rivera. Part of the reason my father stopped believing in God was because Faith, his wife, my mother, had died. With her gone, there was no reason to believe in anything anymore. At least in his eyes.

"Dad," I said softly. His eyes were misting with tears as he stared at nothing ahead.

He leaned on the screen door, distant now, undoubtedly thinking of my mother. "What does she mean?" My father's voice was filled with pain, tightened with burden as he spoke. The angry drunken man who answered the door was gone. Just the sound of my mother's name could sober my father in an instant.

"I... I told her what Mom told me a few days before she passed. There was a scripture she read to me," I recalled. I could see her so clearly, sitting in a hospital bed, weak and withering away. Yet her eyes were filled with determination, not to beat the illness eating away at her, but the illness she knew would one day eat away at me and at my father: Grief.

"There's a time to cry and a time to laugh. Sorrows are going to come but so is happiness and joy. She'd told me there was a cycle to everything, and even though sorrows are heading your way, we don't have to be consumed by them."

"Or stay in the valley," Connie added.

My father's vision locked on Constance, and she said, "Yea tho I walk through the valley of the shadow of death, I will fear no evil. We only walk through the valley. We never *stay*." Connie gave my father a gentle smile. "The only time we stay anywhere is at the end of that scripture, we'll live forever in the Kingdom of God. Which means a valley, a hard time, is only a journey, but *joy*—that's eternity."

After a chilling moment where my Dad battled the tears that'd nearly become waterfalls, he cleared his throat as he turned to me. "You think she can replace Faith, but she can't. No one can."

"Dad," my voice cracked under the pressure of his growing fury. His sadness was leaving to be replaced by misguided grief, and a severely broken heart that masked the pain with anger. I only knew because I'd done the same. "How could you think that? Constance isn't Mom's replacement—"

"Get off my porch, and don't ever come back here." His stare cut me down to a stump. I thought I'd stay frozen on his porch another year when he backed into the dimly lit house and slammed the door closed.

"Keem…" Connie's hand was in mine now. Her warmth brought me back to life as I took a deep breath and glanced at her. "Let's go."

"He didn't mean it," I said as we walked down the stairs. "He couldn't have meant it."

"I know."

"I'm sorry."

"No." She shook her head, and we stopped right in front of the car. "I'm sorry. I think I said too much."

Connie stepped into my embrace; my arms rested around her shoulders as I looked out at the neighborhood before me. Kenny had been telling me that I wasn't part of this place anymore. I was picking up a silver spoon to eat off now. I'd been denying his words, desperately fighting to be part of this place, but as I looked out, I couldn't figure out why.

I didn't belong here anymore; this wasn't my life. All the time I'd spent here had become one far off memory that would eventually turn into a scattered dream. They were pieces across my memory, never to be tethered together again because they'd been broken by the only person tying me to this place: my father.

"Connie," I said quietly.

"Yes?" Her voice was muffled as she spoke against my chest.

"Let's go home."

"Yes, let's go."

19

Constance

"Alright," Vivian said, flipping through the folder in her hand. She was reading over some information as we all settled into my living room. Keem had cooked an array of desserts and an amazing empanada casserole. I'd never heard of it, but the taste made me wish I had earlier. I would've binged this stuff every weekend back in college if I had known it existed.

"I have some very good news today," Viv continued. "We have been cordially invited to the fall B2B Convention, and we are being recognized as the hottest new emerging business of the event."

"What!?" Keesha snapped. "Are you kidding me? Business to business?" She glanced around the room to see if we were as excited as she was. Viv and Gavin were happy. But I wasn't, and neither was Keem—but he didn't know what was going on, so his reaction technically didn't count.

"How are you not excited?" Viv asked as she snapped the folder shut.

"I've been to these things a million times, been honored in every category, twice." I shrugged. "They're only inviting me because they want in on the drama and it looks good to pick my side after Danny's blow out with The Palace."

Kiki sighed and tossed her hands up. "You love to ruin a good mood."

"I'm sorry, Kee," I whined, throwing my arms around her. She shook her head, but I held on anyway and said, "What do they want us to do?"

"Just attend the event and set up a display of our business." Viv quickly scanned the paperwork.

"Well, that's still good," Gavin chimed in as he bit into a peach, "we can acquire more business this way."

"It's a display," I said, "not a sign-up sheet in a college cafeteria. And we're in the new business category. No one does business with the new guys."

"You're clearly in love with mood ruining," Keesha said as she pushed me off.

"Kiki, don't go." I grabbed her arm.

She frowned at me before rolling her eyes and grabbing another fruit tart from the tray Keem had made. "You better count your blessings that I like you," she teased as she sat back down with me.

"I think it sounds good," Keem said from across the room. He was leaning in the doorway, arms folded over a firm chest, muscles hollering in their sleeveless freedom for me to notice them... how could I not?? His lean frame looked perfect, only outclassed by his serious gaze, which was suddenly focused on me.

Keem and I hadn't called ourselves official by any means, but we'd been spending more time together, and he kisses me more often now. I'm not sure if we're ready to put a title on things, but at least for now this was working for us.

"Despite what Connie says," he pushed off the door with a smirk aimed at me, "these conventions are great for new businesses."

"How would you know, Keem?" I tossed at him.

"I heard it somewhere." He shrugged before disappearing into the kitchen.

I rolled my eyes.

Two nights ago, I told Joaquin a story about my very first visit to one of these conventions. Danny had gone too, of course, and we'd hustled that entire event, earning over two thousand contacts combined. We came back and converted eighty percent of those contacts into clients who were already in a legal battle and wanted terms reworked. The other twenty percent was split into two categories; people who didn't respond, and people who'd put us on notice if they needed us. In the coming months, for the half who put us on notice, about thirty percent actually came through. But surprisingly enough, we'd caused enough of a buzz surrounding our growing business, and we had a one hundred percent conversion rate on the half who didn't initially want our services.

So, I knew Keem wanted me to go. He thought it was a good idea because of that incredible story. His telling smirk confirmed that he knew I would give in to his vote.

Reluctantly, I recanted my previous statement with a grumble, "It does help new businesses."

"Wait," Viv said as Gavin passed her a glass of water, "I thought you just said it *doesn't* help?"

"I said that because I didn't want to go."

Keesha laughed and threw her arm around me. "So, this means we're going?"

"Yes," I exhaled.

"Excellent!" Viv exclaimed, her flowing skirt bouncing with her sudden excitement. "I'll make arrangements. We've only got three days to pack so—"

"*Three* days?" Keesha and I said at the same time.

"What's in three days?" Keem was back in the doorway, munching on something from the kitchen. He had a thing about not eating what the chef cooked, despite my rule to have him eat *with* me. We always shared meals; he ate something different from the main course. I think Keem just liked cooking and didn't mind trying all the fresh ingredients and sourced ingredients from different countries that I kept in my pantry.

"The convention," Gavin answered with a shrug. "That's a tight window for flights, and hotels. Especially since hotels are probably booked everywhere nearby."

"Not to worry," Viv said slyly. "Since we're an honored guest, we've got a block of rooms reserved for our team."

"How many rooms?" I asked.

"Four."

I grunted. "We're not *honored guests*. Someone must've

backed out at the last minute and we're the runner ups."

"Why do you say that?" Keesha asked as she reached for another fruit tart.

"Because an honored guest always gets *six* rooms, and they get to pick their room block. Plus, we've got a late invite. We're runner ups or we're leftovers whom they pitied and decided to pick a side in the drama."

"Ouch," Gavin said after a tense moment of silence.

"Well, it's still an opportunity," Keem said. "And you shouldn't pass it up. Isn't this what you wanted, Candy?"

"*Candy?*" Kesha whipped her vision to me so quickly I didn't get the chance to shoot Joaquin a scolding look.

"He meant *Connie*. Right, Keem?"

His smirk widened like I'd issued him a challenge, not asked a simple question. A hand in his pocket, a glide to his stroll; Joaquin crossed the room like the ground carried him to me, and he reached out and lifted my chin. "No, you're my little piece of candy." He leaned closer and whispered, "The sweetness of my life."

"OOOH!" Kesha exclaimed before his words even registered in my mind.

"Goodness, Keem," Gavin chuckled, "you just made my boss crack a smile like I've never seen before."

Keem glanced off at Gavin just long enough to pass him a smile before he redirected his attention to me. Gavin said I was smiling, but I had no idea what to *feel*. Keem just basically confessed to liking me in front of my colleagues. Well ... I guess at this point everyone in this room is a close friend, if not family. Still, it was embarrassing. But even more embarrassing was my childish reaction and inability to resist his charm.

With his hand still on my chin, he leaned down to kiss me. I was sweating now.

From my peripheral, I knew Keesha was smiling, and Gavin and Viv were watching intently. But my focus was on Keem. He wanted to do this, to make things official in front of everyone. I wanted to push him away, to tell him that he'd gone too far. Yet, I sat there. Welcoming him to me, never looking away as he leaned forward… and stopped.

His phone rang, and the entire moment was gone. Everyone groaned in anguish as he retracted with a laugh. "Sorry," he waved a hand, "I just…" he stopped and stared at his phone. Panic had captured his features as he looked up at me. "I've got to take this." He turned on his heels and jetted from the room.

"Is everything alright?" Viv asked in his wake.

I wasn't really listening anymore. Keem hardly ever got phone calls outside of a few call-backs for interviews. We'd been waiting to hear back from a few small businesses he'd applied to, but the look of worry on his face had said something else entirely. It'd said that call he'd gotten had nothing to do with a job interview.

"Connie," Kiki's voice pulled me back from my spinning thoughts, "go check on him."

I nodded and immediately left.

In the kitchen, Keem's phone was left on the counter, and his hands were gripping the edge of it as he hung his head.

"Joaquin?" I said cautiously, not knowing what to expect. I'd never seen him like this.

He looked up immediately, tears were brimming in his eyes, making me afraid to hear what he had to say. Something had gone terribly wrong, and Keem was doing all he could to hold it together. I had to do the same.

"My father—" he gulped, pressing a fist to his mouth to keep from breaking down.

The words burned with instant fear.

"He's in the ICU," Keem forced the words out. "He had a stroke because of a blood clot. Shelley called me, and said he started slurring his words before passing out on their way home from the grocery store. She rushed him to the hospital and staff began administering a dissolvent, but we don't know how much damage the stroke has done yet."

This was the worst news to take in. Swallowing, I tried to pretend I was alright, but I wasn't. I knew how much Keem loved his father even though they'd been fighting for a while. Over me.

"I'll clean up here, and then meet you at the hospital," I said. "You should go see him."

"Is that alright?" His voice cracked louder than my heart.

I moved over to him, and before I could even reach out to touch Joaquin, he'd fallen against me. Squeezing me tight with worry.

"You're all he has, Keem. You have to go," I told him.

"I'm sorry," he whispered.

"Don't be. Just go."

He nodded and pulled away, but not before issuing me a thank-you and kissing my cheek. Then he grabbed his phone from the counter and disappeared from the kitchen.

With wobbly legs, I carried myself back to the living room where multiple sets of eyes were waiting for me.

"What's wrong?" Keesha immediately shot to her feet and bolted over to me.

"His father was rushed to the hospital—to the intensive care unit."

"Oh my goodness." Vivian covered her mouth as she lowered herself to a seat. Gavin was beside her right away, rubbing small circles on her back.

"What happened to him?" Kiki asked.

"He passed out on the way home. He was rushed to the hospital." I paused, nearly choking on the information. "There was a blood clot in his brain that led to a stroke." I could feel the tears swelling, my eyes burning, my chest tightening. Keem's father was all he had left despite them being on bad terms.

Keesha lowered her head, and I couldn't see past my tears to know what Viv and Gavin were doing, but the silence in the room was enough to drive someone insane. Keem was trying to be strong, but I knew he was worried—distraught even, and he should be. He lost his mother, and to lose his father too was more than anyone should have to bear.

"What are we going to do?" Gavin's voice was shy, but he

was asking the obvious question.

Though Keem wasn't part of the business team, there was no doubt I'd been expecting him to go with us. But now, with his father in the hospital, I wasn't sure what to do. No matter how much I hated conventions, I knew they *were* good for business, new or old. Attending would guarantee us at least a handful of new clients, but going and having an award presented confirmed a steady flow of business for the next six months. And if you've got the favor of God, plus some grit, you can turn six months of customers into prospering business like my old one.

Relationships, trust, and good deals were all anyone was looking for in this world. We've been blessed with an opportunity, but personally, I've been blessed to meet Keem.

Since we've met, he's been by my side. Defending me, caring for me, listening and helping me. Now, he's in a time of need. He needs me to be there with him. Could I really walk away from this for my business?

I sniffled, wiping at my tears. "You guys go to the convention. Keem and I will stay back."

"But, Ms. Wells," Gavin said, "without you, no one's going to—"

"They will," I nodded at Gavin, "they'll be interested to know why I didn't attend. The mystery alone will drive clients our way. When they find out it has to do with Keem, they'll eat that up." I tried to smile, but even I knew I was fooling myself.

How long can drama float me along until I'd have to grab serious high-paying clients who couldn't care less about my personal issues? No one will take us seriously if I don't go, but I can't leave Keem. Not now.

"There's no need to make a decision yet," Keesha said. "Let's call it a day for now. Viv, let them know we're coming and leave it at that."

Vivian nodded as she stood, Gavin interlocked his fingers with hers and the two left the house.

"What do I do, Kee?" I asked once we were alone. "This is an opportunity for my business, but Keem..."

Keesha sighed. "You're worried about him, aren't you?"

"Yeah. I just feel like I owe him. He's been there for me, and to just leave and go to this convention. It doesn't feel right."

"I know. I can't make any decisions for you because you're in such a tight spot. But I'll tell you this; Keem is understanding, the business world is not. We've been praying for an opportunity; we can't just let this pass. We're talking *millions*, Connie." She stopped to chew her lip. It was a hard conversation for both of us. Keesha knew how much Keem and this business meant to me. Which loss was I willing to take was the question. A business loss or a personal loss.

"This business isn't just about you, Connie," Keesha reminded me. "We're *all* working for you. We *all* need a job. And with the small fry deals we've been bringing in, we *all* won't last much longer."

"So you want to just forget Joaquin after everything?"

"I just want you to remember that this is bigger than just Joaquin."

"But I…" I stopped and clutched my chest.

Too soon, I thought.

"I know you mean well, Kee," I said, after a heartbeat of tense silence. "I'm grateful for everyone who has stood by my side through all of this. But if you swapped places with Keem and needed me to stay behind …" I looked her right in the eye. "You know for a fact that I would."

"You know for a fact that I would never ask you to stay."

Until now, I hadn't realized how much this all meant to Keesha. She was my best friend who'd joined my new business to help me get out of a divorcee slump. But now it's turning into something real. Something with a serious shot at success. And, to her, it feels like I'm the only one who doesn't see that or care to see it.

"You know as good as I know that he won't ask me to stay," I said. "You know the real problem I'm having is with myself."

"Do you love him?"

"Keesha—"

"If you can't immediately answer yes, then go upstairs and pack your bags. We've got a trip in three days."

She turned to leave, but I followed behind her.

"You can't be serious, Keesha?"

"I am!" She whirled around. Her face was stricken with guilt, and anguish. She was as twisted as I was, but she knew someone needed to talk sense into me, and the look in her eyes was enough to convince me.

"I'm sorry," I said, dropping my gaze to the floor. "I'll be ready to go in three days."

She paused, then her voice came out softer than before. "Constance, I didn't mean to be so—"

"It's alright." I grabbed the front door and opened it. "You've done enough for me, Kee. I've got to figure this one out on my own."

20

Joaquín

The monitors beeped as my father lay asleep in his bed. The doctors told Shelley and me they were monitoring his reaction to the dissolvent. So far, there'd been no side effects, but they wanted to continue to monitor him. As of now, the MRI scans showed there was minor damage from the stroke. My dad will likely walk away from this with just a slur to his speech. It was a miracle, and nothing less.

"Hey," Shelley said as she sat beside me. Taking my hand in hers, she squeezed it.

"Hey," I whispered.

"I'm going to head home soon; you should go home too and get some sleep."

I shook my head and sighed slowly. "I can't leave him, Shells, not again."

"This isn't your fault."

"I should've been there."

"Keem—"

"He almost died while I was off doing—" I tossed my hands up, and the words came out quietly. "Kissing a girl in a mansion."

"Living your life apart from your father is exactly what he wanted. He wanted better for you, Keem, but he knew you'd never go for it if you stayed there with him."

"What?" I reflexively clutched her hand, and she glanced down.

"That hurts."

"Sorry."

"Listen, Keem, this is probably something your father should tell you himself when he wakes up." She stood and patted my shoulder. "I'll be back tomorrow." Shelley left me there in the room with a new blow to the gut.

My father wanted me to leave, and I was an idiot and actually left. I should've known he just wanted me to go live a fresh new life. His anger toward me hadn't even made much sense but I'd accepted it and moved out.

Was I being stubborn? I could admit my ego had been bruised when my father asked me to leave, but our relationship had already been strained before that. I really thought he'd just been looking for a reason to put me out and grabbed at the first remotely bad thing I'd done.

"Dad," I whispered as I leaned forward and grabbed his hand, "I'm so sorry. I'm such an idiot."

The door to his room opened, and Constance walked in with a bouquet of flowers. I hadn't seen her since yesterday when I first got the phone call. She told me she'd come later, but I hadn't even noticed she wasn't here. I've been so engulfed with thoughts of my father, fear that the medicine they gave him won't clear the clot, or worse, cause some bad reaction. I didn't even check in on Connie when she was a no show.

"Hey," she said quietly as she came and sat beside me, where Shelly had been sitting not long ago.

"Hey, Constance. I'm sorry I didn't call or come home. I should've—"

"Don't apologize." She set her flowers down on the table beside my father and sat again. "I was going to call you yesterday, but I figured you'd be caught up here and I didn't want to interrupt."

"I wasn't too busy." I reached for her hand. "I would've answered."

"I know. That's why I decided not to call. And it's why I've decided not to go to the convention."

"What? Connie, you have to go. I'm not even part of the company, I'm just your…" I stopped. I didn't have a clue what I was to Connie. All the time we've spent together, the kisses, the stories, the dates, Constance and I had never mentioned what we were.

"How's your dad?" she asked, changing the subject.

"He's doing alright. They're monitoring him to make sure the medicine they gave him doesn't cause any other problems. And they're monitoring his blood pressure, hoping it'll go down soon."

"And his brain, is he alright?"

"You'd never believe it." I glanced back at my sleeping

father. "They said slurred speech may be the only thing he has once he wakes up."

"What!? Oh, thank Jesus. That's so good, Keem!" She sighed and dropped her head. "I was so worried."

"Hey," I lifted her chin, almost shocked to see tears in her eyes, "it's going to be okay."

Pulling her chin from my grasp, she shook her head. "I'm sorry. I'm supposed to be helping you, being strong for *you* for once. And I can't stop myself from crying."

"Connie," I murmured as I pulled her close, "every single tear you shed for me makes me want to be a little closer to you. Your tears make me stronger."

"How?" She sniffled against my chest.

"Because I know I have to get that much stronger to protect you from the reason for these tears. If I'm strong enough to protect you from the hurt, then you'll always be happy, and so will I."

She fell silent. There was much to discuss, but I didn't know how to bring anything up. I knew what I felt for Constance wasn't just a crush or a hormonal misjudgment. What I felt for Connie was real. I needed to be by her side. I needed to protect her. I needed to love her, because if I didn't, I'd lose myself.

Constance was everything I wanted. She was beautiful, and she was kind and strong, though she didn't know her own strength. But beyond what I wanted; she was who I *needed*. Someone who kept me focused on Christ for both of us and loved Him as I did. Someone who cared for my wellbeing, and someone who wanted me to succeed.

My entire job hunt has been so different this time compared to last time. Sure, I've got a cozy spot, and even if I get a good paying job, it wouldn't compare to Connie's billions. But the hunt to provide for her was welcomed. It wasn't the challenge of finding a good enough gig to pay her bills—mostly because I knew I wouldn't find one with my skill set—it was *her*.

Constance Wells made everything in my life better. I hated job hunting when my dad got me in good with Mr. Adams. But for Connie and *with* Connie, I've enjoyed every moment. Been on the edge of my seat as I've been waiting to hear back from anywhere.

After everything we've been through, the times we've shared, my affection for Connie grew. I've tried to ignore the way her smile makes me nervous, and the way I can't ease up on this job search. I've tried to ignore how much changing that house around for her meant to me. I've tried to ignore everything good, but then I'd be ignoring *everything*, because Connie was a gift to me from God, and I knew it. She's an answer to my mother's prayer, that I'd find someone when she passed on... that I'd find someone to love.

"Constance," I whispered. She'd fallen asleep, resting peacefully in my embrace. How long had we been tangled up like this? We'd adjusted our position so I was sitting in the comfy chair and she was on my lap. But at the sound of her soft snoring, I realized just how much time had passed.

She was here for me, making the most of this situation,

giving up a business opportunity to stay by my side. I couldn't let her career go down the drain for me. These past few months have been hard getting Connie's faith back and getting her strength back. She's strong enough to do this now, and I can't rob her of that.

"Connie," I whispered again. She groaned and adjusted against me. "I think we need to talk."

"About what?" she answered drowsily.

"About us."

The words were like a key to a lock. She was suddenly lively, and the drowsiness began to fade as she sat up and fluffed her curly hair. Smooth brown skin, glossed lips, and a beauty that was otherworldly. Connie and I had an obvious gap between us. Not just in age, but in careers, even lifestyles and the way we'd grown up. But I was willing to close the gap.

"What do you want to talk about?" she asked.

"I want you to go on that business trip."

She frowned. "Why? Don't you want me here?"

"More than you know. But I want you to go and figure out an answer to a question I have." I forced myself to maintain eye contact with her as I asked, "Connie, do you love me?"

She didn't gasp, or blush. Her reaction was rigid. She stiffened, *literally*. Her back straightened and the frown she'd been holding only tightened. Constance didn't look angry. She just looked confused, like the question had never crossed her mind. I was hoping that confusion was because she loved me and had never thought of us in any other way *except* lovers. However, I knew better.

Constance Wells was a twenty-seven-year-old divorcee who just recently stopped loving her ex-husband. She's barely been able to move on. She just got strong enough to mention his name without exploding into tears. Ms. Wells has struggled to love herself; how could I possibly think that in a few short months she would love *me*?

I fell in love with Connie by accident. I was just returning her car when I noticed she was beautiful. I was just sharing a scripture when I realized she was broken and needed support. I was just wearing a fancy suit and holding up my end of a deal when I realized she was scared. And I was just coming to a friend's house when I realized that Constance Wells was unloved—she didn't even love herself.

Every instance between us melted my heart for her. I didn't realize I was in love with Connie until I couldn't stop fixing that house. I worked day and night when I wasn't working a shift at The Palace. When I saw the destruction she'd caused, heard the treacherous tale that went along with her outrage, I couldn't stop working. Restoration, that's what I promised myself to bring her. But instead, I ended up falling in love with her and brought her a loaded question with all kinds of implications on her own silver platter since—well—I probably couldn't afford a silver platter.

"You don't have to answer." I tried to ease the tension in the room. "But I want you to at least consider the question while you're gone. And when you come back, if your answer is no, I will accept it. I'll still be your chef, and I'll still be right by your side."

"Then it doesn't matter what my answer is, does it? You're going to stay by my side either way, so why ask me this?"

"Because I need to know who you want me to be in your life."

She blinked at me, eyes quickly roving over me before she stood and leaned in to kiss me. It was so emotional, so painful, feeling the burst of emotion from her strawberry gloss against my lips. She was kissing me, breathing heavily as she tried to contain herself in the hospital room. I wasn't trying though. I was kissing her like a teenage idiot trying to convince his girlfriend that it wasn't about the sex—trying to show her that he really loved her. And I did. I really loved Constance Wells, and I'd do anything to prove that.

When she pulled away, we were breathless. Panting as we left our desire on each other's lips.

"I'll go, but when I return, my answer won't be any different than the one I'd give you today."

Grabbing her things, she prepared to go, but I caught her hand and kissed it. "I love you, Constance."

Her lips pressed into a flat line before she nodded and slipped her hand from mine.

I watched her leave the room in silence.

"I thought she'd never leave but seeing that made the wait worth it."

My eyes shot to my father who was smiling in bed.

"Dad...?"

He laughed as he tried to sit up. I rushed to his side and hit the button on the bed, so it would lift for him.

"Dad, are you okay? How are you feeling?"

He waved me off like I was annoying him, and I suddenly remembered we were technically still feuding.

"I'm fine," he slurred. Thick hands grabbed the sheets as he said, "I'm glad you're here, Keem."

I tried not to get emotional, so instead of speaking, I gave him a quick nod and moved back to my chair. We didn't speak for a while as my father rested. He was just staring ahead, and I was staring at him, wondering how he felt, wondering how much he remembered. His face was eternally cramped, his speeches slurred like he'd been drinking, but his quiet demeanor told a different story than when he became a crazy drunk.

"Joaquin," he started, "we need to talk."

"I know," I said as I adjusted in the chair. "I'm sorry for what happened, Dad. I shouldn't have left. I should've been here for you."

He looked over at me, a plaintive look on his face. His thick Spanish curls were wild like usual, and sunburned brown skin sagged in some places over my father's short frame. My parents always wondered where I'd gotten my height from, but I'm certain my mother's grandfather was tall from the pictures I've seen.

"Keem, let me start from the beginning," my father said. "Shelley and I were arguing, and all of a sudden, my speech started sounding funny. And the next thing I know, you're in here kissing that woman."

"I can explain."

"Nope," he raised a hand, "I've still got more to say. I'll start from the actual beginning this time."

Slowly, I nodded while he sighed and licked his lips.

"I ain't doing too well," he confessed. "And I haven't been doing too well for a while now."

"What are you talking about?"

"This ain't the first blood clot."

I squinted. "Dad, there's no way you've had others. We lived together, remember?"

He nodded. "When you were still there, I got one in my leg. It wasn't too serious, but I had Shelley tell you I was passed out upstairs and didn't want to be bothered. And like a good obedient son, you never bothered me. Though I knew it was because you hated to see me drunk."

I ran an anxious hand over my hair. "Dad, this can't—"

"Let me finish," he grunted. "The doctors told me at that visit that I didn't have much time left. The alcohol had fried my liver, and my health had taken a turn for the worst." He sighed like he was defeated and tired of fighting. "I didn't want to die knowing I never did nothin' to make your life better. I couldn't go out like that. So, when the time finally came and I was gettin' worse, I put you out."

I shook my head, refusing to believe that Shelley had told me the truth. She had no reason to lie, but I wished she had.

"But it was in that loneliness after you left, that I finally found the strength to reach out to God again. I've been angry for a long time," my father said. "Angry I couldn't protect your mother. Angry at God while angry at myself for being angry at

God." He chuckled. "And I was angry that, in the midst of all this, I'd lost you. My drinking had pushed you away, but I was too much of a coward to own that, and so I drank until it killed me."

"Dad," I snapped.

He threw up his hands and shrugged. "Joaquin, I'm not going to make it."

"*No.*" There was a lump in my throat, and a thousand bricks sitting on my chest, threatening to crush it and break my heart. "I can't lose you too."

"You're going to lose me, and I want you to be prepared for it."

"Stop it!" I snapped. "How can you be so calm?"

"Because I've had eighteen months to figure this out, get all my ducks in order, and I have, Keem. The only thing that was missing was my faith. But you helped me find my hope in God again. You, and Constance."

I stared at him, tears dribbling from my chin onto my shirt. I didn't care, I wasn't thinking. I was about to lose the rest of my little family, a little dampness down my shirt didn't matter.

"When you two showed up," Dad was smiling now as he recalled the time Connie and I came to the house to grab a few things I'd left behind when I moved out. "I did everything I could to be angry at you. But that was easy, because I was angry at myself, so I just directed it at you, and at Constance." His eyes found mine, lazily blinking. "You looked like a man. Finally. A happy one, and I knew that everything was going to be alright. I'd found my faith again, and my son was finally happy again. I could leave this earth today and know I've done something right."

"You can't leave me!" I cried as I lunged forward and hugged him. "Dad, please don't leave me."

He patted my arm as I cried over him. "You're strong, Keem, and I'm so proud of you. Falling in love is a beautiful thing, son."

"You can't just die." I broke free from him. "You can't just leave me with nothing! What about Shelley? And the house?"

"Shelley moved out last month. She only comes to visit me to see how I'm doing since the clotting had gotten worse. And I'm in the process of selling the house. I was going to bag up your mother's things and send them to Constance, hoping she'd give them to you."

"And *me*?" I shrugged and sniffled at the same time. "What about *me*? Were you going to say goodbye?"

He shook his head. "I couldn't. I didn't want you worrying or troubling yourself with me. You've got plenty of life to live with that wonderful woman."

"How could you make a decision like that without even consulting me?"

"Keem, it was for your own good."

"It was for *your* own good!"

Silence.

"You're right." His chuckle wasn't filled with amusement like it had been earlier. Through the slurred words and the strong front, there was pain in my father's goodbye. "It was for my own good, avoiding a goodbye with you. But I'm glad I got to see you again, Keem. I'm glad I got to see you happy and in love. Now I'll get to tell Faith that you're alright."

I pressed my hands over my face. "Is this really goodbye? Do I seriously have to send off another parent?"

"No parent wants to be buried by their child. But what is the alternative? To bury *you* instead?" He grimaced. "Really, no parent wants to be buried at all. I want to see you grow old like me, but I've got to be responsible for my decisions."

"We can pray, and God can reverse all of this!" I said desperately. "I believe He can."

Dad shook his head. "I've accepted this, Keem. I know God can heal me from head to toe if I just ask Him. But I've made peace with God, and I can't wait to see Heaven and your mother. I wish I could've done a lot of things differently, but I don't wish for more time. You're going to be alright, Joaquin."

"How can I be alright? I'll have no one," I whispered as I stared down at my shoes. Tears plopped to the ground between my feet.

"You'll only be alone if you stop believing in God, and if you let Constance go through that convention by herself."

"Dad, this is not the time—"

"*Listen* to me," he said sternly. Though his speech was slurred, the intimidation was very present. "You found a woman you love. Go and get her. Don't let her walk away and hope that she'll come back. Chase her down and marry the woman."

I shook my head. "I can't believe you're giving out advice

in this predicament."

"Joaquin, I just want to see you happy. And Constance makes you very happy. Stop thinking about everyone else and think about you just for a second."

"How can I stop thinking about you? You're dying and you've accepted that. There's nothing I can do."

"The only thing you can do is be happy. I'll make one promise to you. I'll be here when you get back from that convention."

"I'm not going," I refused. "I'm staying here, by your side. I can't afford to miss any more time with you."

He yawned and sank into his pillows. "I'll be here when you get back, Joaquin. You need to be *there*, not here."

"I can't... I can't go. I can't leave you."

My father nodded.

"What?" I snapped.

"You're not that worried about me."

"Yes, I am!"

"You're worried that she won't say it."

I choked on my response, coughing and gagging until I grabbed a water bottle and desperately drank a few sips. My father sat in bed, laughing his head off like he didn't have to keep his blood pressure low.

"Sitting here with a dying old man is not going to get you the answer you're looking for. Go home, freshen up, and surprise her with a marriage proposal," he said in Spanish now. I was grateful he switched languages because his Spanish wasn't so slurred, maybe because he could speak it better than

English.

"Dad, I'm not popping the question without knowing if she loves me. And I can't think about that right now."

He chuckled. "God's given you the chance of a lifetime. Are you seriously about to lose out on a billionaire princess because of me? I told you, I ain't going nowhere until you come back. Now, what's it going to be, Keem?"

I rushed a hand through my hair and rested my elbows on my knees. "I ... I don't know."

21

Constance

"You showed up at the airport when we were boarding without telling us you were even coming. Then, you flew in silence. I get it, you don't want everyone to know your business. But then you get here and you're still handing out the silent treatment?" Keesha tsked me and crossed her arms. "I don't think so. We're in blistering hot Arizona with nothing to do but stare at the cacti until the convention starts tomorrow. So, you wanna tell me something?"

I sighed as I flopped onto the bed in my hotel room. "There's nothing to tell, Kee."

"Oh please!" Viv grabbed a pillow and gently smacked my back with it. "I'm not buying that."

"Not you too, Viv."

"I'm so invested in this relationship." Kiki laughed and clapped as she agreed with Vivian.

"There's nothing to tell," I insisted. "Joaquin's father was ill, and so we took this space to think about some things. That's all."

"Things like what?"

"Things like *things*." I shrugged. "Gosh, Viv, lay off." I pulled the pillow from her and laid back on the bed. I'd done everything I could to avoid thinking of Joaquin and his question, but my friends wouldn't let it go.

"Come on," Keesha pulled on the pillow, "you can't leave us hanging."

"Yeah! We need to talk about this," Viv agreed.

"How about we talk about you and Gavin instead, Vivian?" I questioned.

"What's there to talk about? Gavin and I love each other. What more is there to say? If you want to talk about his accountant brother's wife, then sure. But they're clearly in love, and everyone is upfront about their feelings. I don't get why it's so hard for you and Keem."

"I know," Keesha agreed. "She's so clammed up about Keem."

"Is it because of Danny?" Viv asked.

"Wow," I whispered.

"That was too far!" Kee barked.

"I'm sorry!"

"No." I sat up. "That was the first time someone mentioned Danny and I didn't have any kind of reaction. Not even an uptick in my heart rate."

Keesha's face lit up as she nearly killed me in a suffocating embrace.

"Oh my goodness! I can't believe it!"

"Me either," I whispered. When Kee finally let go, I said, "Daniel was my first love, he was my husband. And I just never thought," I paused, but Viv filled in the blank with her best guess.

"You never thought someone else could love you?"

"No..." I shook my head, a small smile capturing my lips as realization set in. "I never thought I'd love someone again."

The squeals that ensued was enough to drive me crazy.

...*...

The first two days of the convention were busy. There were all sorts of people here this time. The convention got bigger every year, but I'm sure this had to be the biggest one yet. Tables lined every wall, and every corner of the four buildings rented out were filled with businesses and people. All the work kept my head straight. I banned Viv and Kee from mentioning Joaquin until we returned home so I could focus. I wondered how he was doing but refused to text him. He hadn't reached out to me either, but I figured things with his father kept his attention, and he was probably giving me space to consider his feelings, and mine.

Today was the last day of the convention, and it was going to be the best day for us. We'd be able to bring in a ton more businesses we hadn't reached yet with our display and table setup.

Gavin and Vivian were still working the crowds as Kiki and I worked the table. We were getting swamped. People handed us business cards, asked us questions, showed me old photos of Danny and me, asking for a signature. Some showed me the magazine covers with Keem and me from our date at The Palace and begged for a signature. The day was busy to say the least, but it had been even more successful than we'd planned.

When the day began to wind down, there were still a few stragglers walking the long halls of the once tightly packed space.

"Phew," Keesha said as we began to pack up, "how many do you think we got today? All these little businesses are taking over. There were hardly any big businesses today."

"I know." I nodded as I folded our tablecloth. "Even in the thriving business category there were only a hundred and fifty big names out of the thousands that were here today. It used to be the other way around. A handful of entrepreneurs and then big businesses left and right."

"But the world has changed," Kee said. "Entrepreneurs have the same options all the other businesses have."

"Not just the resources, but they've got the drive these old guys had when they were first starting. With all the resources available to entrepreneurs now, can you imagine how different the world will be in thirty years?"

Keesha stopped packing up our promotional packets and nodded. "If Steve Jobs had the resources and capital to build a PC as easily as your average gamer can now, along with all the legality that keeps people from stealing each other's work, Apple would be in iPhone three thousand by now."

I snorted. "I think you're right. The only problem is that there was one Steve Jobs, one Bill Gates, one of everything. The world won't survive with a million Steve Jobs making the same product."

"Nah." Keesha wrinkled her nose as she packed. "The world will do the process of selection. Survival of the fittest. The top dog will still come out on top. There'll be a bunch of cheap knockoffs, but still only one iPhone."

"You're absolutely right."

"Connie?"

I turned, and every ounce of joy I'd been feeling from the convention was instantaneously sapped away.

"Daniel…" his name was but a whisper on my lips.

Jada was on his arm, of course. She always acted like she'd won some secret competition with me when in reality, she was having my used seconds. There was absolutely no competition, at least not anymore.

"Keesha." Danny nodded at my best friend.

"Daniel," she said darkly, and her eyes fleeted to Jada. "Tramp."

"Excuse me!"

"Keesha!" I snapped.

"I'm sorry." She threw her hands up and walked away. "I can't deal with them."

Sighing, I looked over at a fuming Jada and silent Danny, but then I noticed he hadn't defended Jada. Usually, he came running to her aid, but today, he didn't say a word.

When Keesha was gone, Danny exhaled and said, "What

are your plans tonight? Let's do dinner."

"I'm sorry, Daniel, but I—"

"Come on, Connie, what's the harm? Just dinner for you, Jada, and me. We can talk business."

"Funny," I said, "you want to talk now."

He raised a brow, but only licked his lips and nodded. "Jada and I will be at Holly's Wood. We've got a nice cozy booth. Stop by."

I glanced over at Jada who was still fuming. I wasn't sure if she was angry at Keesha—though she was right to be—or if she was angry that Danny had just invited his ex-wife, whom he stiffed out of the marriage, to dinner with them.

"I'll see what I can do."

He nodded, dark cheeks pulled back into a grin. It was the first time he'd smiled since he walked over. Danny wasn't being his usual sly and demeaning self. He was quiet and reserved. Maybe it was because of all the drama surrounding us. This dinner was likely a way to smooth things over between our businesses. There'd be no doubt if I attended this dinner tonight with him, it'd be smeared all over the news.

When they finally left, I took a deep breath. I had time to think about Keem now. If I went to this dinner, there'd be all kinds of implications. And when it all got back to Joaquin, what would he think? I didn't want him to be angry about it, I didn't want him to think that I came here and forgot about him. And I definitely didn't want him thinking that dinner with Danny was my answer to his question.

Going tonight would prove one thing to myself; that I am

in love with Joaquin Rivera.

You'd think it'd be the total opposite. Going to dinner with my ex-husband and his fiancée would mean I was desperate and didn't care about Keem. But that's just not true. When Joaquin ran to my house in the middle of the night and stayed all night, even after he'd worked double shifts because I was crying, that was when things began to change for me. My feelings for Keem were being choked out by my desperation for Danny.

What Viv said was true, I never thought someone would love me again. Not the way I thought Danny had. But it turns out, someone does love me, and they've loved me better than anyone else.

God is amazing. I've been to The Palace countless times, and never noticed the valet workers, and I'm certain they didn't pay me much attention because I frequented it so much. Plus, there are so many *actual* celebrities who visit The Palace. But God had Keem there, a kind natured young man with the world in his eyes, to rescue me from the spiraling downfall I was about to send myself into. And from that day, my life hasn't been the same.

I love Joaquin and tomorrow, when I return home, I'm going to tell him. But first, I had to make it through dinner with Danny and set some things right.

...*...

Gavin and Vivian showed up as I finished packing up the table and they took over for me so I could run out and grab a dress and take care of a few errands before dinner. I hadn't packed anything fancy enough for dinner with my ex-husband, and I knew cameras would be clicking away like crazy at this dinner, so I had to look good. Thankfully, I'd be home before the magazines hit the printers, so I'd be able to fully explain the dinner to Keem before he saw it in the tabloids.

"Where are you going?" Keesha asked as I stepped out the bathroom. Grabbing an envelope and my clutch, I headed for the door in a sweeping red gown.

"I'm going to dinner."

"Like that?"

"Yes."

"With whom?" She crossed her arms.

I raised my chin. "With Danny and Jada."

"You're kidding me. I just called that girl a tramp! Got all ungodly with her—and you're going to dinner with her and your ex-husband? What about Keem?"

I twisted the doorknob and looked back at her with a smile. "This *is* for Keem."

I walked through the hall, watching all the couples enjoying the live entertainment. This place looked no different from high school, which was almost comedic. People in their basic nature just wanted to be happy, but they had no idea *how* to be happy. A drink in hand gives them the confidence they need to make a move. But if they had God, they'd have the boldness of a lion ready to hunt its prey and unafraid of animals twice its size. They'd have joy that only comes from God, and not fleeing moments that come with lowered inhibitions that, apparently no one ever remembers. So, I beg the question, why drink if you won't even remember?

Deep thinking and walking was not a good idea. I walked right into a woman in a long orange gown that flowed with each one of her movements and made it look like she was engulfed in a flame.

"Sorry," I said quickly, and as the woman turned to respond, I recognized her. "Brianna Gem? From Gem Jewelers?"

She smiled and offered her hand. "It's Mrs. Ackard now."

I glanced at the tall and handsome man standing beside her. A dark suit and his long hair pulled neatly into a bun made him look divine. They were close in age, and they looked like it. Keem and I weren't, and hopefully we *didn't* look like it.

Clearing my throat, I inclined my head to Mr. Ackard, "When did this happen?"

"A year or so ago." Brianna beamed with joy and pride.

"That was right after that big jewelry event where I sold you back my engagement ring right?" I asked.

She laughed. "Yes, we got married soon after that."

"Wow... Congratulations."

"Thank you so much, Constance."

"Well, I've got to go to dinner. Sorry again for bumping into you. I was lost in thought."

She waved a brown hand like there wasn't a single problem in the world. Could it be that love brought that kind of happiness? Could it be that love founded in the principles of

God released His promised joy? It was no small matter that Mr. and Mrs. Ackard were Believers. Since Keem and I were as well, I had high hopes for our future together, despite our age difference. Joaquin had always made up for that with his intelligence and maturity, so I wasn't worried at all.

"Have a good evening," Mr. Ackard said as I moved past them.

I gave them a wave and headed through the crowd and into the restaurant.

I found Danny and Jada sitting at a table; he was reading the menu, and she was sipping a cola. They weren't speaking, or even looking at each other. Seeing them be so distant was odd, but I let the thought roll off my shoulders because I didn't care about the state of their relationship. I'd come to this dinner for one reason.

"Evening," I said as I stood at the table.

Danny looked up, his eyes growing bright as he saw me. For a fraction of a second, I swear he was gawking at me like the first time he met me years ago.

"E-Evening," he said, flustered.

Jada quirked a brow. "Are you suddenly ill? You've seen her before," she snapped.

Danny was barely able to take his eyes off me when he turned to Jada to offer her an apology. "Sorry, baby, I thought she wasn't coming."

Jada rolled her eyes, but never even looked up at me.

"Jada," I called, "can you give Danny and me a moment to talk business?"

She frowned. "Can you give Danny and *me* a moment without you nearly ruining our lives? You've been nothing but trouble for us since—"

"Jada," Danny's voice grew dangerously quiet, "give us a minute. It's just business."

With a huff, Jada scooted out the booth, revealing a skintight dress that showed off her big pregnant belly. When she stormed off, I took a seat across from Danny.

"Constance," he reached across the table and grabbed my hand, "I didn't know you missed me as much as I missed you. When I heard that you came alone, I knew I had to see you."

His words bounced around the noisy room as I stared at his hand on mine. Holly's Wood had an old time feel to it. Like an old Hollywood movie, but the movie was based on cooking over a woodburning stove. Logs were strategically set around the restaurant as décor, the walls were made of bricks, and there was even a little movie set for people to take pictures at.

"Danny," I said, still staring at our hands. "What in the world are you doing?"

"Come on, Connie," he bit his lip and leaned closer, "you want me to beg? Even though I know we're *both* dying to see each other again. Let's not make things complicated. Mistakes were made, tensions flared, but we always bounce back, baby."

"You cheated on me," I said flatly. "For years. We could never bounce back." I ripped my hand from his. "And I'm not your *baby*."

Frustrated, he nodded and shrugged. "So why are you here wasting my time?"

"When you held my hand, my skin crawled," I said.

The look of astonishment on his face was to die for.

"You thought I'd cave for you because I'm so desperate. Typical Daniel." I shook my head as I set the envelope on the table. "That's the rest of the money I owe you from the divorce. We're officially over, Daniel. Don't ever speak to me again." I straightened my back. "And don't you ever lay a finger on Joaquin again."

The next second, he was across the table, gripping my wrist, nearly lifting me out of my seat. All kinds of attention turned toward us as he yanked me closer to sneer in my face, "Who do you think you're talking to? I will *destroy* you, Constance."

I opened my mouth to snap a hot reply at him when a calmness broke through the storm.

"Am I interrupting something?"

When I glanced up, my heart almost ripped through my chest in excitement. "Joaquin," I breathed.

He was wearing a suit, all black with a crisp white button down and no tie. There was a chain around his neck that was visible since the first few buttons on his shirt were open. A diamond watch on his wrist, and a gentle smile on his charming face. Reaching out, he took my other hand, and I stood from the booth as Danny let me go.

"I came to give him severance pay," I quickly explained. "It was all the money I still owed on the divorce."

Keem nodded.

"I realized something, Joaquin."

"What's that?" he asked softly.

"That my answer truly didn't change. I was able to face Danny, all by myself, and I didn't break." I got choked up as Joaquin swiped a hair from my face.

"I'm so proud of you, Constance."

"Joaquin, I love you."

"Good." He slipped a hand behind my back, the confidence that always closed the gap between us was there again. "Because I love you too, and I came all the way here to marry you."

He leaned forward and pressed his lips over mine without even waiting for an answer. But he hadn't questioned me. Joaquin came here to marry me, and without hesitation, I will.

I thought I'd never be happy again, that Danny had taken everything from me. But as we kissed, right there in front of the entire convention, in front of my ex-husband, I realized that God had used Joaquin to restore what was lost.

It was better than ever before. Love I had never known to exist was finally mine. And this time, it was real.

Epilogue

Joaquín

1.5 years later

"Hey, Mom. Hey, Dad," I said, setting flowers into their vases. "It's been a crazy year and a half. I miss you guys a lot; wish you two could've been at my wedding to see Constance. She looked amazing walking down the aisle." I paused and glanced over at my father's grave. I could imagine him making some kind of crude joke about our wedding night and I laughed to myself.

Dad passed shortly after Connie and I returned from the Business to Business Convention. His body started rejecting the medicine, and he had another clot in his brain. He'd kept his word; he was there when I returned. But eventually, he passed on, and I was left with no one but God and Constance.

"She's been my anchor, keeping me tethered to God." I exhaled slowly as I read their graves, side by side. "How does she look, Dad? Does Mom look great?"

He'd always told me that he couldn't wait to die to see Mom again. It was a super morbid thought, but now, as I looked at their graves, I actually felt a smile tugging at my lips. They were reunited, and it was the only thing that brought me peace in this storm.

It took me six months after my father's funeral to return to their graves. Connie's been coming faithfully every month with or without me.

I leaned down and cleaned some dirt off Dad's grave. "We got married, and went on our honeymoon, and now I'm finally moving into Constance's home. She also hired me. I'm still her personal chef on the weekends, but I actually have a nine-to-five job at her company now. That Business-to-Business convention really was good for us, just like Gavin said it would be."

We ended up raking in a lot of smaller businesses at the convention. By winning their trust and their cases, Connie's new business began taking the reins of the deal-making industry. Danny's business, the one he tried to steal from Connie, fell apart. Jada left him after claims over the paternity of her baby began to circulate.

Danny's a fighter, or maybe he's just stubborn. He's still trying to compete with us even though there is no competition. Daniel's business is failing, and in the next six months or so, I'm sure we'll be getting calls about someone wanting to buy his business and what kind of deal we could work out for them.

"I'm Connie's secretary now," I told my parents. "Vivian was made an official partner of the company, and so was

Keesha, who passed off the head of marketing to Gavin. And last week, Gavin finally proposed to Viv; she said yes, of course." I smiled. "The two of them seem really happy together, so I'm glad it all worked out."

Lowering myself to the ground, my eyes traced between the two gravestones. I couldn't believe that losing everything had brought me a life better than I'd ever imagined. Losing Mom opened a door for Mr. Adams to hire me because he pitied my dad. Working at The Palace, I bumped into the love of my life. Sharing a scripture with her, she ended up falling for me and we both shared the Gospel with my father. Before my father passed, in his weakened state, he gave me the courage I needed to ask Constance to marry me.

If you looked at my life, you could easily raise a fist to God and blame Him for all the pain. But the Bible is the Truth, and I believe every word in it. Because weeping endures for the night; but no matter how long it may seem, it's still only a night. Joy does come in the morning.

Not the evening, or five days later. The moment the sun breaks through the clouds, joy is rising on its rays. And I know for certain that though my season of mourning was horrifying, this new season I'm in, this season of dancing, I'm afraid my legs will soon fail me from all the twirling. There's something to celebrate every day, and I'm so grateful that God blessed my mother to teach me to endure. To teach me to remember God's Word is the Truth, because the mourning has passed, and the morning of joy has come.

I stood to my feet and glanced out at the sun peeking

through the clouds as it rose. The mornings were always my favorite time to visit my parents. It was so peaceful, blanketed in an unusual feeling of bliss, despite the mounds of graves everywhere.

God had been right. Jesus had spoken the Truth in the church that day. He'd used me to draw my father back to Him; and in the end, everything had worked out in my favor. I'd gotten what I'd wanted. My parents reunited, my dad rediscovered God before he passed, and I fell in love. I didn't fail my mother; I became someone, and was able to keep living after losing her, and after losing my father.

"I'm happy," I whispered as tears burned my eyes. "Constance is happy, and she's so much stronger now." A chuckle escaped me as my breath danced on the howling wind. "For whatever reason, God thought I'd match best with a billionaire divorcee. It's funny, His plans are totally not ours."

As I crossed the graveyard, a thought bloomed in my head, making me laugh. I shoved my hands into my pockets and trucked over the crunching morning frost that held the grass captive. The thought of seeing Constance kept me warm and the thought of our strange love story kept me smiling.

Gaps existed in every aspect of our relationship. From our age to our jobs to even our faith, at one point. But we managed... well, really, God intervened. A valet kid from the ghetto fell in love with a billionaire and, thankfully, she loved him back.

The End.

More books by A. Bean & TRC Publishing!

Christian Romance
The Living Water
Withered Rose Trilogy
Fractured Diamond
The Woof Pack Trilogy
Singlehood
Beautiful Lies

Christian Fantasy
Cross Academy
The Scribe

Christian Post-Apocalyptic Fiction
The Barren Fields
The End of the World series
MAGOG saga

Christian Science Fiction
I AM MAN series

Christian Romance
The Living Water
Withered Rose Trilogy
Fractured Diamond
The Woof Pack Trilogy
Singlehood

Christian Children's Fiction
<u>Too Young</u>

ACKNOWLEDGEMENTS

Thank you, Jesus, for blessing me with another idea; I hope I made You proud.
Thanks for reading. This story was one of my favorites to write.
Let's do this again sometime.
Until then.

The Rebel Christian Publishing

We are an independent Christian publishing company focused on fantasy, science fiction, and romantic reads. Visit therebelchristian.com to check out our books or click the titles below!

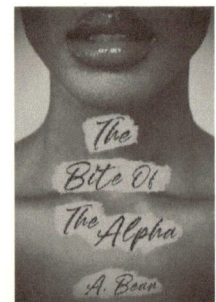

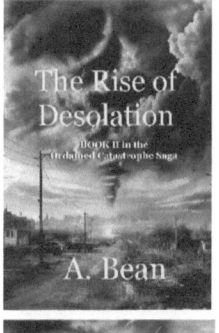

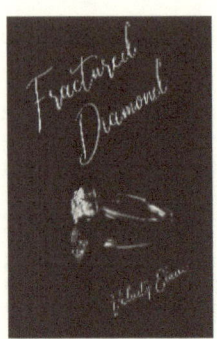  
  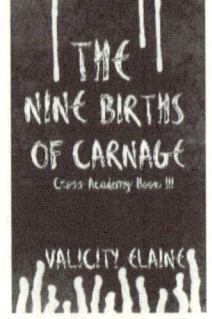
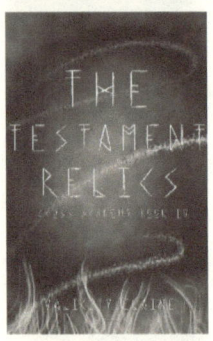  
  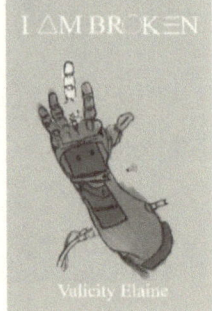

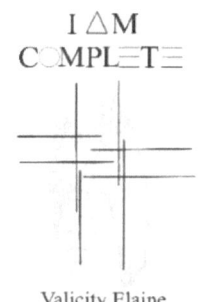

Made in United States
Troutdale, OR
04/20/2025

30756033R00152